CHRISTMAS WISHES IN WILD HARBOR

GRACE WORTHINGTON

WELCOME TO WILD HARBOR

I'd love to send you free bonus epilogues both now and in the future that take place in Wild Harbor. But you can only get them when you join my newsletter list.

You'll get notified of sales on my books and other great deals.

Get Lily and Alex's bonus wedding epilogue at graceworthington.com.

Enjoy!

CHAPTER ONE

MILA

The bride posed in the three-way mirror, shifting her body from front to back so that she could glimpse her figure from every angle.

The dress shimmered in the light, the hand-sewn beading flashing with every turn.

Olivia fiddled with the neckline, pulling the gown up to cover her well-endowed chest. "I'm not sure, Mother. Do you think this dress is the one? I like it, but I only get to choose one dress and I want to make sure I choose the right one."

This bride had been particularly fussy, trying on over a hundred elaborate gowns before she declared this one the perfect dress.

The seamstress had altered the dress to her measurements perfectly, fitting her every curve without an extra inch to spare. But now her forehead wrinkled like two perfectly sewn seams were threaded through it.

Mila folded her hands together calmly as she watched this

saga unfold. This could only mean one thing. The bride was not pleased.

"I'm not sure about it." The bride continued to twirl with a dissatisfied pout that was an obvious distress signal for her mother.

"What is it, darling?" The mother hustled to her side and began circling her back with her palm. "Olivia, is it how it fits? Does it not feel right?"

Brides' mothers were always subject to an enormous level of stress. After all, they were attempting the impossible: creating their daughter's dream-come-true wedding. This typically resulted in high levels of anxiety bubbling over into every single decision, including the all-important choice of a gown.

Olivia's brow deepened. "I'm just wondering if I should go with a full gown instead of a fitted one."

Susan Smith continued to pat her daughter's back as if this was an impending crisis. "Maybe we should go back to the drawing board and try on more dresses. What do you say, sweetheart? We are spending thousands on this dress. We want to get it right."

Mila cleared her throat gently to remind them that she was still in the room. She attempted a cool, unaffected face punctuated by a reassuring smile. She'd dealt with brides like this before. Young women who couldn't decide on a dress, no matter how many they tried on. She was like a preschooler playing in a pile of dress-up clothes. All her hopes and dreams were placed on the dress, expecting it to magically transform her from an ordinary young woman in jeans and a T-shirt to a fairy-tale princess.

"I understand you're having second thoughts about the dress." Mila used her most soothing voice, a soft, pillowy tone that sounded like something between a psychotherapist's question and a children's lullaby. She needed to strike a balance between reassuring the bride and understanding her concerns. Her business reputation was counting on it.

Mila knelt down and fanned out the train of the dress so that it draped around the bride for a perfect photo finish. The result was critical to a final decision.

"This dress is spectacular on you." Mila swept over the bride's body. "Look at your gorgeous figure. The shimmer of the satin. The hand-sewn details. Now that it's been altered, it highlights your waist and draws the eye to your face. We'll see all the love and radiance you are feeling on your wedding day. You will be the most beautiful bride ever!"

She was going overboard, but some women needed the lavish praise when making a final decision. Otherwise, they would never make up their minds, always flip-flopping between multiple gowns, wondering if the perfect dress existed in the world.

It didn't exist, but Mila wasn't about to explain that. She owned the wedding-dress shop, and her job was to make every bride feel exceedingly special, unique, beautiful.

Convincing the bride to say yes to the dress was the only way she made money. Plus, there was the sticky issue of the refund policy. No dress could be returned after it had been altered. It was a term of the contract that Mila avoided mentioning unless forced to.

Olivia softened under Mila's extravagant praise. "I do like this one." She turned in the mirror some more, checking out her backside. "But is it the perfect one? I'm not sure."

Mila was hoping the bride wouldn't waffle. Because the dress had been altered to her exact measurements, if they backed out now, they'd lose their deposit.

Since the gowns were designer brands, each worth thousands of dollars, Mila ended up taking a hit when a bride backed out. The only thing she could do now was gently remind the bride of her nonrefundable deposit and hope they'd keep the dress.

Mila adjusted the delicate lace strap on the bride's shoulder. "I think this dress looks like it was made for you. After seeing you in dozens of dresses, I can't imagine a more extraordinary choice for your special day."

It was easy to make a woman feel good. Mila had no problem envisioning how beautiful each bride could be on her wedding day. She didn't have to stretch the truth. Every woman was extraordinary in her own way.

The bride beamed under the praise, then her brow furrowed again. "I'd like to see a few more dresses. Ones with Cinderella skirts. Lots of pouf, like a dress made for a ball!"

Mila kept her smile pasted on but was left with no choice. "We'd be happy to show you more dresses, but you've already paid the deposit for this dress, and unfortunately, there are no refunds for that down payment. However, we can let you make a deposit on a new dress, if that is what you want."

"What?" Susan nearly choked on the words. "I thought we could apply that deposit to any dress we chose." Her forehead crinkled like a piece of aluminum foil.

Mila folded her hands together, a picture of calm, like the Mona Lisa. "Since the dress has already been altered to her exact measurements, we need to pay the seamstress. That is why the deposit is nonrefundable. Not to mention the dress will be harder to sell since it's been fitted."

"What do you mean I don't get my deposit back?" Olivia's furrowed brow turned into a scowl that matched her mother's. Neither was happy with this arrangement. The bride turned to her mother, her eyes glossy with emotion. "Mother, I have to have the right dress!"

"We'll get the right dress. Yes, we will, princess." Susan patted her daughter's spine before strutting over to Mila with angry eyes. "We need to take care of this. Now."

Mila had dealt with emotional bridezillas before—and their equally pushy mothers. Everyone was under so much stress that it was difficult to defuse the situation. Nobody enjoyed paying more than they had to, but Mila knew she couldn't keep her shop open unless she had these terms. She'd made the mistake of being too lax before, and the price she'd paid was closing her first shop in her hometown. Now that she had reopened a different store in Chicago, her terms were set. It was a careful balance that made it hard for the pickiest of brides.

Mila's hands remained neatly folded, a placid smile at the corner of her lips. She was the epitome of calm, even if her insides were quaking under the pressure. "If this is not the one, I'm happy to assist and help the bride find a wedding dress of her dreams as long as the terms are understood. So, shall we move forward and look at more dresses?"

Olivia wiped tears from the corners of her eyes, trying not to ruin her fake eyelashes.

"Of course," Susan cooed, rubbing her daughter's back as if she'd just endured a traumatic moment. "Where shall we begin?"

The bride's face blossomed into a full smile. "Oh, thank you! I want to try on as many as possible!"

Mila's lips twitched, but she resisted the urge to claim a victory just yet. After all, the bride was still undecided. "Let me call my assistant, Hadley, and we'll bring you as many dresses as you'd like."

The bride jumped up and down in her gown, clapping her hands, her brown curls bouncing like ping-pong balls.

Mila stepped out of the dressing room and let out a slow exhale of air, like a balloon with a pinprick hole. Susan didn't balk at losing her deposit and the bride was elated to look for an alternative. Hadn't she just saved a precarious situation?

Of course, there was still the bride's altered gown, which would need to be sold at a discount. All things considered, the situation was still successfully resolved with no screaming matches between mother and daughter. In the end, if the bride was satisfied, that was all that mattered. Every dress eventually found its owner like a happy match.

Except in Mila's case, her own wedding dress still hung in her closet. Unused. Untouched. A sad reminder of a broken engagement, buried deep in the back of her closet. She blinked away the white-hot image.

Mila stepped into the back room, where Hadley was unpacking a new pale pink gown. "We need you in the dressing area. A bridal emergency."

Hadley raised her eyebrows. "One of those days, huh?"

Mila nodded, then returned to the dressing room where the bride still admired herself in the mirror.

Hadley poked her head in. "How can I help?" The young assistant had worked at her shop for only a brief time but had become a lifesaver for Mila.

"Yes, bring out a selection of dresses with full skirts for our lovely bride. Size eight."

Her assistant's face twitched as her eyes flitted over the bride's dress. Hadley knew better than to ask. She'd get the story from Mila when they closed the shop.

"Of course. More dresses coming right up."

Olivia stepped into a private dressing room to change, leaving the mother of the bride and Mila alone.

An undercurrent of tension thrummed like a bass guitar string. "Do you need anything while you wait? Otherwise, I'll help Hadley choose some beautiful gowns."

Susan's eyes turned hard as flint. "No." They flitted over Mila's hands clasped at her waist, zeroing in on her fingers. A tiny smile formed on the woman's thin, pursed lips. "I see you aren't married."

Mila could feel her shoulders tighten at the mention of her missing engagement ring. The lady's smile wasn't a token of friendliness, but something more sinister.

"No, I'm not, Mrs. Smith."

"Hmm. Interesting. It's hard to find a good man these days unless you have everything going for you. Olivia was so very lucky to meet her fiancé at her university. I've heard that if you don't find a man by the time you're in your mid-twenties, it's an uphill battle. Virtually impossible. Not that you can't, but you know, dear, all the good ones are taken."

Mila was almost twenty-seven, just over the mid-twenties hump, apparently an old maid by Susan Smith's standards. Was this her way of getting back at her for keeping the deposit?

Mila caught her reflection in the three-way mirror, like a house of mirrors. The terror in her face cut through her frozen expression. "Yes, I'm sure your daughter and her fiancé will make a good couple." She was trying to divert the conversation, but it was so difficult to allow this woman to slice the knife through her.

Mrs. Smith wouldn't let it go. "I just thought it odd. Someone who sells wedding dresses and can't find a man for herself. Does it drive you crazy to see beautiful women trying on your dresses, when you haven't had the chance to?"

She wasn't about to explain to Susan Smith that she had a dress. A very lovely gown hanging in her apartment right now. Mila chose her words carefully. "It brings me great joy to make my brides happy."

Susan gave her a spiteful glance of satisfaction. "Well, then."

Mila glided to the door, still emanating a yoga-calm vibe as her heart pounded violently. "If you don't mind, I'm going to help my assistant."

When she closed the door behind her, she tipped her chin toward the ceiling, trying to stem the tears in her eyes. She would not let this lady get under her skin.

Most of the mothers weren't this difficult. More often, they were cotton candy sweet, women who wore cardigans and smelled like pumpkin-spice lattes. Suburban moms who had sacrificed countless hours at ball practices and swim meets. The kind of mother Mila had, soft and sweet, like a chewy caramel square.

But on rare occasions, she experienced the dark side of wedding planning, butting heads with overbearing mothers who carried cross expressions like they were martyrs on a sacred quest. They couldn't be satisfied. Not one bit.

Since opening her first shop fresh out of college, Mila had never had a customer who had found her weak spot so easily or quickly. It's not that she minded the single life. She quite enjoyed the freedom with its flexibility to come home at any hour or skip dinner. But when people assumed she wasn't fit to be married, it picked at a wound she'd thought had healed over.

Her scar was an empty finger on her left hand.

She went to the showroom, where Hadley had already picked out a dozen dresses.

"Boy, she's a peach," Hadley whispered.

Mila glanced over her shoulder to make sure they were alone. "The mom or the bride?"

"I was referring to the bride. Throwing a fit over her dress? It looks gorgeous, like it was made for her. Adrienne did a wonderful job on the alteration."

"My professional opinion is that she's suffering from decision fatigue. When you've had too many choices, then you start to second-guess yourself. It's a problem with brides."

"I thought she was gown-obsessed. The type that likes to play dress-up."

"Have you talked to her mother?"

"No, why?"

"She noticed I wasn't wearing a ring and made a jab about me being single. Like it was a criticism as a wedding-shop owner." Mila pulled out a puffy dress with lots of tulle, like a giant marshmallow.

Hadley rolled her eyes. "That low blow all because of a

deposit? She probably has more wealth than I could ever dream of."

Mila held up a lacy skirt that billowed like a parachute. It had a gigantic skirt. "It comes with the territory. Stressed-out brides. Stressed-out mothers. They attack everyone because they need to take it out on some unsuspecting person, right?"

"I'm sorry, Mila." Hadley scrunched her face in dismay.

"I appreciate the sympathy." She'd be fine. She was always fine, right? Never mind that this woman had twisted a fishhook in her raw wound.

Mila should have been married by now, but a year ago, everything had fallen apart. Embarrassment hovered over her like an invisible cloak. The wedding-shop owner who couldn't keep a man. It still stung.

Mila hung a dress with enormous ruffles on a rolling garment rack. Her shoulder throbbed from lifting the heavy gown. She rubbed the sore spot and tried to stretch her neck to one side. A pain shot down the length of her arm.

Hadley slid gowns down the rack to make more space, while the decadently fat skirts fought for room. "Is your shoulder hurting again? Do you want me to take over with this fitting? Let the mom use me as a punching bag." Hadley lifted her fists and gave a swift roundhouse kick in the air. The carefree exuberance of youth gleamed off her smooth, rosy cheeks.

"You don't have to do that. I'm fine, like an old punching bag that doesn't even feel the kicks anymore. I just wish I could take some time off." Mila stretched her arms in the air so that her petite frame gained an inch of height. Any more stretching and her spine would snap.

"Seriously, you need a break. You've been working so hard for the past several months. Why don't you take some vacation over the holidays? I only have one family event on Christmas Day, so I don't mind working extra."

Mila waved her hand in the air. "No, no. I couldn't let you do that."

Hadley was a golden employee, putting in extra time, even when she wasn't getting paid. Mila couldn't figure out how she had gotten so lucky. Especially since her last employee had cheated her out of significant money.

An extended Christmas vacation sounded divine, but could her dwindling bank account afford it? The thought floated through her mind like the soft flutter of a leaf falling. Hadley was clueless about the financial struggles the shop was facing. Mila had only casually mentioned a few paycheck delays, and Hadley had always responded with a casual wave of her hand. "That's fine. Whenever you get around to it," she chimed, like this was nothing more than a blip on the radar instead of a giant storm approaching.

Mila had struck gold with such a dedicated employee who didn't seem to have a dishonest bone in her body. Hadley had the beautiful ignorance that defined a recent college grad—still hopeful that life would simply work out as planned. It wasn't any surprise that she carried a starry-eyed gleam. Hadley lived with her parents and enjoyed their financial safety net. It simply didn't occur to her that life could come tumbling down with one disastrous turn.

But Mila knew better. Her life seemed to crumble like a sandcastle. No matter how she tried to pat the sand back into place, it just kept slipping through her fingers.

Only a few months before, she had made a devastating decision. Her last employee, Stacy, had needed a temporary loan after going through a messy divorce. Mila couldn't stand on the sidelines and watch this girl's life fall apart. Grams had taught her that when people needed help, you pitched in like an Amish barn raising. The whole agreement seemed innocent enough: Give her an advance on several paychecks, and Stacy wouldn't be evicted. She could always pay Mila back later.

Then, without warning, Stacy hadn't shown up for work one day. When Mila had called, she had already switched phone numbers and left town. Later, she'd found out that Stacy had not only taken the money Mila had advanced her, she had also withdrawn a large sum from the business savings account. How could Mila be so dumb? She trusted that people were good, but just like her imaginary sandcastle that kept slipping away, her trust in people was slowly eroding.

She stared at the stacks of bills lying on her desk in neat piles, ominous reminders that she needed this month to be extra profitable or she'd have to make major cuts in the new year. She'd fight closing the store at all costs.

The vibration of her cell phone jolted her back to the present. Thelma Ratcliffe's number flashed across the screen. "Hey, Grams!"

"How's my big-city granddaughter doing?"

"Surviving . . . barely." Mila's tone was light and jovial, but there was a tiny hairline crack under the surface.

"When will you be home? I've hardly seen you." This was Grams's way of trying to twist her arm. An old-fashioned guilt trip.

"I'll be attending Lily Woods's wedding in a week. Didn't Mom tell you? We're celebrating Christmas that weekend too. It's a bit early, given it's the middle of December."

"Yes, but that's not enough time with you. What about Christmas Day? I haven't made my holiday fruitcake yet. You love my strawberry jam." Her treats were staples at their family's Christmas celebration.

"I will miss it desperately. Can you mail me some? I'll eat it alone around the Christmas tree thinking of you and all the delightful memories of home."

"Humph." Grams didn't hide her feelings. Her disapproval was like the frown on a kindergartner's drawing. "Why don't you just stay until Christmas? Or do you not like me?" She could imagine Grams's hint of mischief sparkling in her eyes. She had this pointed, funny schtick down. Humor was her vehicle for truth, and it hit Mila right where it hurt.

"More than anything, I want to be home for Christmas. But I have to get more sales in this month." She sat on the edge of her desk and flipped through her bills, dread creeping up her spine. She could make the three-hour trip on Christmas Day if the weather cooperated. That was a big *if* since both Chicago and Wild Harbor were known for their lake-effect snow squalls.

"Why not have your assistant take over while you go home for Christmas? You're the boss." Grams was a take-charge kind of woman. She'd always run Gramps's life like a drill sergeant before he passed away, and he was happy to let her. It was a win-win for both of them.

"There's only one problem. I can't pay her right now." Grams was squeezing the truth out of her like a lemon. Taking more time off wouldn't help a business that was barely making any progress.

"How are you ever going to meet a man if you never have any time off?" Grams was keenly interested in Mila's dating life, which was nonexistent since her breakup with Jake. Mila had buried herself in work, trying to keep her wedding shop afloat. Meeting a man was last on her list of priorities right now.

"I guess I'm just going to be a sassy single woman like you, Grams." Mila cracked a grin behind her phone. She could dish it out as much as Grams could.

"I might be sassy, but I don't want to be single for long. I'm on this newfangled senior citizen's dating app, and I'm planning on meeting Mr. Right as soon as I get a new profile picture on there."

Mila knew Grams loved Gramps more than anything, but she wasn't one to wallow in her grief for long. Time wasn't on Grams's side, and she wanted to spoil another man with her affection again. Mila understood what it was like to feel time slipping through your hands.

"How do you know if you haven't met him yet?" Mila couldn't imagine her grams on a dating app, explaining what traits she wanted in a man. Gramps had seemed so simple on the surface, like an oversized teddy bear. She couldn't picture Grams with anyone else.

"I feel it in my bones. But it might be my arthritis too." She knew Grams was humoring her, trying to soften her up for dating advice. Grams had been begging her to return to Wild Harbor ever since she moved to Chicago.

"Do you have a hot date for the wedding yet?" Grams tried not to sound overly interested, but Mila knew she was fishing for some juicy gossip.

"I'm not planning on going with anyone." Mila opened another envelope, her thumb sliding neatly along the seam as it split in two. She pulled out another bill. *Overdue.* She laid it on the urgent pile.

"You know Jake has a new girl."

The words twisted her stomach into knots, even though she tried to let them slide right off. She needed thick skin, like a cement block wall. "I really don't care to know who Jake is dating."

"Why don't you find someone you can have fun with? Nothing serious. Kind of like prom."

"I didn't even enjoy prom." Mila's high school date had been a friend from calculus class. Instead of making small talk, he'd stared at the other couples and blundered through a few math jokes. A decent-looking kid with the personality of a butcher block.

"I don't know. I'm not looking for fun."

"You sound like the saddest country song I know. Let me give you some help. What if I pay your assistant so you can take some extra time off? Oh, and I'll pay your bills this month too, so you don't have to fret about that."

It's like Grams knew about her financial troubles without even asking. "I couldn't possibly let you do that."

"I'll take it out of your inheritance. Consider it a loan with one catch."

"Is there something behind this?" Mila couldn't help but fall for the bait. She desperately needed a loan and a vacation, and her grandma had dangled the carrot, luring her into a bargain.

"You find a date for Lily's wedding."

How in the world would she do that? She was too busy to have a dating life, much less try to meet a man. She didn't even know where to look for one. She had known Jake since high school. Where do you meet a kind, decent bachelor when you worked with brides?

"That sounds impossible." Mila felt the walls of her office squeeze in, like they were about to crush the life out of her. She stood quickly and knocked the bills off her desk. They fluttered to the ground like a flock of paper birds. She knelt to pick them up, the amount due flashing like fire, burning her up, until she was a husk. On her hands and knees, her shoulder cramped painfully. There was no way she could pay these. Even with the best sales month ever, she would still be in debt.

"You just think about it, honey." Grams let the pause hang in between them. "You don't even have to tell me ahead of time. You show up with a date, someone you want to be with, and I'll loan you the money."

Mila sat back against her desk on the floor, a pile of insurmountable bills in her lap. One date and she could start the new year fresh. A shiny prospect of hope dangling like a worm on a hook.

She scrunched her legs to her chest and propped her elbows on her knees. "I'll think about it. But I'm not making any promises."

"You know I'm not asking you to find a husband. It's one date. At some point, you just gotta get back on the horse."

"Horse. Gotcha. I'll see you at the wedding. Guest or not. I'll let it be a surprise."

"And if you find a man my age, I'll gladly take him. Surprise me, honey."

A corner of Mila's mouth curved. "A date for me *and* you? That's a big wish. Although I'm sure I'd have more luck finding someone for you."

Grams laughed, then said goodbye.

All she had to do was find a date. How hard could that be? Mila groaned and put her head in her hands. From where she sat on the floor of her office, the walls still felt stifling, but they were no longer squeezing her like a vise. Grams had given her a way out of this mess.

She hadn't been planning on staying more than three days. But now that Hadley had offered to work, and Grams had made her an irresistible offer, the idea spun in her mind like a wobbly top.

It had been so long since she hadn't worked herself to the bone. Her life was wedding dresses. What would she even do with herself? Time off in idyllic Wild Harbor sounded like a bite of luscious pie.

Her phone rang again. Mila stood and adjusted her skirt. Back to professional Mila. Not desperate Mila making split-second bargains with her grandma.

"Hello, this is Mila Sutton."

"Mila, this is Lily Woods. Do you have a minute?"

"How's the bride-to-be?" Mila relaxed her shoulders. Ever since kindergarten, Lily's sister, Cassidy, had been Mila's best friend—practically another sister. *Inseparable* was how their elementary teacher had described them. Hearing her voice made Mila wish she was already home.

"Okay, I think?" Lily's voice was friendly, but pinched. "I'm so sorry to bother you. I'm sure you're swamped today."

"I have a few minutes. What's up?"

"I've got wedding-dress jitters. I'm afraid it won't fit."

"Lily, your wedding dress is perfect and ready to go. I'm sure it will be fine."

"But what if it isn't? I've gained a few pounds from too many treats this month. I had this nightmare last night that I couldn't even fit into my dress."

Ah, yes. *The bride's nightmare.* Other brides had mentioned that disturbing dream. Usually, in the dream, they had to don their regular clothes or their undergarments. Either option was horrifying.

"Don't worry. You're entirely normal. Every bride I know stress-eats. Adrienne usually gives a little breathing room from the measurements."

"But what if it's not enough? Those buttons on the back won't fasten otherwise. Should I diet this week just to be sure?"

"Don't do that. Yo-yo diets aren't great for your health. I'll be out the day before the wedding to make sure it fits."

"You said Adrienne gives some extra room in the dress?"

"Yep. She doesn't want a bride to feel like she's suffocating in a corset."

"I just wish we had more time." She could hear the worry in Lily's voice.

What if she went up to Wild Harbor a week early? Lily could see if the dress fit, and if it didn't, there would still be time to make a small final adjustment. Plus, it would give her time to decide on Grams's offer and scout the town for a last-minute date. Maybe she could talk one of her high school friends into accompanying her, even though Grams had encouraged her to pick someone she was interested in.

"I have an idea. What if I come home early for your fitting?"

"You don't have to do that. I trust you, Mila. This is your job."

"But wouldn't it ease your mind? My assistant volunteered to work extra over the holidays. Not many brides shop for dresses this time of year anyway, and you don't know how badly I need a break."

Mila heard a loud squeal from the dressing room. Apparently Olivia was having a ball playing dress-up.

She leaned against the wall, her shoulder still sore from her tense muscles. "Now that I think about it, a trip sounds like just what the doctor ordered. What are you doing tonight?"

"Just putting together some table decorations for the reception. But I could work in a dress fitting." Lily sounded relieved already.

"Then it's a done deal. Don't you worry at all. I'll call you when I get close to Wild Harbor."

"I can't believe you'd do this for me."

"For your family, anything." It was true, she loved the Woods family like her own.

As she ended the call, Hadley peeked her head around the corner. "Fingers crossed. I think she found the dress!"

"Oh, good! Whatever we can do to send her off as a happy bride. By the way, I'm taking you up on your offer. As soon as we get the dress settled with our bride, I'm leaving town."

"You mean today? I've never seen you so—"

She didn't want to say it. "Impulsive?"

"Spontaneous. You're usually planned so far in advance, you can't fit anything into your schedule. Not even a night out on the town. I'm proud of you."

She didn't know if anyone had ever used the word spontaneous to describe her. Her life generally followed the same pattern every day. Even her wardrobe was color-coded. Mondays were black-dress day. Tuesdays, navy blazer with white pants. Wednesdays and Thursdays she tried to cheer things up with color—an Ivy League green or a flaming red, while weekends were for patterns. Floral Friday and Striped Saturdays. It all made logical sense.

There was no room for vacation in the pattern of her life. It was an anomaly from what was normal.

"After the last several months, I've realized I desperately need a break. Maybe Olivia and Susan Smith were exactly what I needed—the final push to do something spontaneous, for once."

"Who knows? Maybe you'll even meet someone." Hadley wasn't teasing. She lived for the dream of love. She nearly bubbled over hearing every bride's engagement story.

Mila jotted down a few reminders and grabbed the stack of urgent bills. The clock on the wall was nearing five. Normally, she'd work a few more hours after the store closed on a Saturday, but not today. "Oh, I doubt that. I'm not looking for anyone. He'd have to run into me before I noticed him."

"Never say never." Hadley gave her a wink. "Enjoy every minute."

"I will. Call me if you need anything. I owe you for this, Hadley." Mila plucked her black wool dress coat from the back of a chair and grabbed the garment bag holding Lily's wedding dress. As she stepped into the frigid temperatures, the icy wind stole her breath away.

She walked a block, turned toward the parking garage, and saw a man dressed as Santa standing next to a red kettle.

She fished around in the bottom of her wallet, looking for some cash. She usually only carried credit cards, but she hated walking by a donation bucket empty-handed.

A shiny silver object winked at her from the bottom of her wallet. Her grandfather's silver dollar.

Every year at Christmas, Gramps had gifted her a card containing a shiny coin. When she was seven, she'd declared the new coin her lucky charm and had hidden it in her purse. Over the years, she'd transferred it from purse to purse, eventually forgetting it in the corner of her wallet. She had learned long ago that there was no such thing as luck, but she still couldn't bring herself to toss it.

She dug around in her purse, raking through the bottom, reluctant to give away a memory tied to her gramps, who had passed away a year ago.

Santa clanged his handbell like a clock chiming the hours. "Merry Christmas!" he bellowed in his best Santa-like voice. His beard sat crookedly on his chin while the long white curls of his wig blew into his eyes.

"I'm sorry I don't have more change." She held up the silver coin, giving it a quick goodbye before she held it over the coin slot. Gramps would understand that it was time to let the coin go. Her luck had run out long ago.

The coin clattered at the bottom of the pail.

Santa's face flashed a smile under his fake beard and rosy, frostbitten cheeks. "Thank you, my dear, and may your Christmas wishes come true."

What Santa didn't know was that they already had. She was going home.

CHAPTER TWO

MILA

Mila's legs ached as she saw signs for her hometown of Wild Harbor. Almost home.

As she pulled onto Main Street, a clogged intersection jammed with slow-moving vehicles inched forward. Traffic moved at an irritable crawl.

"This is as bad as Chicago," she muttered to herself.

Even in beach season, the town wasn't this congested. Didn't all the tourists hibernate in the winter months?

A big sign with bold red letters caught her attention. *The Wild Harbor Winter Festival.* Her mom had mentioned the new Christmas festival, but she wasn't expecting a mad rush of people. Lush evergreen boughs swirled down light poles. Wreaths hung around the lanterns, framing them in light. Shop windows glistened with twinkle lights and magnificent fir trees stood at every corner, decked out in silver bulbs. Carolers dressed in Dickensian costumes stood on the corner singing "God Rest Ye Merry, Gentlemen." Snow dusted the ground, framing everything in white. It looked like a scene straight out of a Hallmark movie. No wonder Mila loved her hometown of Wild Harbor, Michigan, so much. The beach had always been a huge draw to tourists given its idyllic location on Lake Michigan, but since moving, she loved her home even more in the fall and winter, when the small town turned into a winter wonderland.

Her phone rang. It was her mom, *again.*

"Hey, Mom. I bet you're calling to ask where I am."

"I thought you were going to be here an hour ago." Diane Sutton's voice echoed with concern.

"I'm stuck in traffic now. But what really slowed me down was the last-minute packing. I'm not great with spontaneity."

"Why'd you come early, then? I hope Grams didn't pressure you."

"It wasn't Grams. Try a Christmas bridezilla who insisted on a new dress. She pushed me off the cliff."

"Oh, sweetie. If your wedding shop was still here, you wouldn't have clients like that. The people in this town don't have exalted expectations." Her mom was still trying to convince her to move back to Wild Harbor. Never mind that she had already tried—and failed—to keep a shop open.

"Mom, there are bridezillas everywhere. When my shop was here, I couldn't make ends meet."

Mila's stomach tightened at the memory of closing her Wild Harbor bridal shop a year ago. Her sales hadn't been great when the cold winter months arrived, but she also couldn't get over the real reason behind her shop's demise. The town couldn't handle a bridal shop owner whose fiancé had dumped her on the day of their ceremony. Her reputation as a jilted bride dogged her every time she returned home.

"How is your shop doing now?" The question was innocent enough, but Mila wasn't about to confess the extent of her financial woes. She had already made that mistake with Grams.

Mila hedged. "Busy." It was the truth. "As long as clients are happy, I'm happy." Her mom knew that money had been stolen from Mila's shop, but she had failed to disclose how much.

"But the traffic in Chicago—" her mother lamented.

"Have you seen Wild Harbor today? I'm sitting in a traffic jam as we speak." A car horn honked behind her. The driver was frustrated she hadn't inched forward.

"But isn't the winter festival gorgeous?" Mom gushed. "A developer in town started it this year. He's the one who took that condemned building on Main Street and turned it into a new coffeehouse."

"French Press Café? You told me about him. I have the feeling he's some hotshot entrepreneur who has his sights set on turning Wild Harbor into a year-round tourist attraction. It's a shame, really. I always loved how quiet this town was in winter."

"I don't think he wants to change the heart of it. He's reinvigorated the town. All the shops and restaurants are full. The weekends are packed—concerts, festivals, and a light display. People like that he's a go-getter, and it doesn't hurt that he's handsome."

"So that's what's swaying you. A good-looking guy who's on a mission to capitalize off of Wild Harbor's greatest asset."

Her mom laughed. "No, I talk to him at the café every week. My book club meets there."

"I never thought I'd see the day you would give up hosting the book club."

"He's the one who invited us. He has a private room for groups, but we like the front table by the window. My friend, Edna, swoons over him. He's a real winner with the older ladies. I should introduce you, Mila."

"Uh, that is kind, but no, thank you. Because I know what you're trying to do, and I don't want to be set up."

"Edna mentioned he's not available, anyway. It appears he's taken to your old classmate, Lexy."

As her car crept forward a few inches, Mila pictured the

petite homecoming queen of Wild Harbor High. They had been good friends until Lexy had started dating Mila's ex-fiancé, Jake, after their breakup. Eventually, the relationship fizzled, but it was too late to repair their friendship.

"She certainly seems to sink her claws into Wild Harbor's eligible bachelors." Mila strained to see if she could find a detour. "Sorry to go, but I need to find an alternate route around this traffic jam. I'm hardly moving. Be home soon."

As soon as Mila ended the call, she remembered a side street that would get her home faster than inching through this traffic jam. She squeezed out of her lane and turned onto a quiet street of well-kept Victorian homes decorated for Christmas. Twinkling lights twined up trees, while fresh evergreen swags draped across painted porches. As she admired the lavish decorations, she turned just in time to see a man on a bicycle crossing directly in front of her in the dark.

Mila jolted as she slammed on her brakes. The man glanced up at the last minute, swerving to avoid her bumper, but it was too late. Her car hit his front tire, and the man tumbled off his bike and rolled to the ground.

"Oh, no!" Mila cried as she slammed her car into park and rushed out to help him, leaving the car door hanging open. Why had she taken her eyes off the road?

"Are you okay?" She knelt beside him as he lifted his head and blinked a few times. His eyelashes were dark and full, a half-moon shadow against his cheeks.

"I'll call for help. I'm so sorry. I didn't see you until you were in front of me." Her voice cracked as she pulled out her phone.

The man shook his head and mumbled something as he slowly raised himself off the ground. One hand drifted to his elbow, where he touched an open gash in his skin and winced.

His face was shadowed with stubble across his jawline and his bike helmet was askew, revealing wavy, dark brown hair peeking out. He unbuckled the strap and pulled it off.

He rubbed his eye, then his gaze drifted to hers. For a brief second, neither said anything. His denim-blue eyes mesmerized her, reminding her of cobalt stone. Delphiniums in June. A peacock's tail.

"Did you hear me?" He cocked his head.

She realized he was speaking to her. "Oh, I'm sorry." She shook her head. Apparently, he'd struck her dumb. How could she have missed seeing a man on a bike? She wasn't blind.

He stretched his arm out, peering at the wound. "I asked if you could cancel the call. I don't need an ambulance."

"Oh, yeah." She hadn't even dialed 911 yet, but was still holding the phone. "You look like you're in pain."

He grimaced as he moved to stand. "Give me a second." He ran his hand through his tousled hair and slowly straightened his spine. "I think I'm okay, but my bike isn't."

Mila glanced at the mangled tire on the bike and her mind replayed the split-second accident. One second, she was admiring decorations, and the next, he was in front of her hood.

"Should I call an ambulance? Are you hurt? Maybe you should lie down until the paramedics get here."

"In the middle of the street? I think that might be more dangerous." His mouth twitched.

Her heart was bouncing around in her chest like a pinball game. "You might have a concussion." Mila squinted her eyes and moved closer to his face. "Or internal bleeding. I don't want you to die on me."

He lifted his eyebrows as his gaze traced her face. "You're really not helping me feel better. But I'm pretty sure I will not die."

The tension in Mila's shoulders eased. She smoothed her hair. Never had she imagined that she'd run into someone on her way home. Like literally run him over.

"I think I'll be fine." He stretched his injured arm out again and grunted in pain. "Maybe."

"I'm so sorry. You appeared out of nowhere." Her week at home had already started out on the wrong foot, all because she hadn't been paying attention.

His face softened as he wiped the dirt off his legs. "Don't beat yourself up. It was my fault for not stopping. There was a car parked on the street, so I couldn't see you. I like to think I'm invincible, but obviously, I should be more careful." He rubbed his jaw. "My name's Max, by the way." He put his hand out to shake hers.

Mila's hand seemed tiny in his massive palm. "I'm Mila. Normally, I would say it's good to meet you, but that feels inappropriate given the circumstances. Sorry we're meeting under these conditions. I never dreamed there would be bikes out in winter."

He patted the damaged tire of his bike. "With my fat tires, I go everywhere unless the weather is bad."

"Can I give you a ride somewhere? Obviously, you were headed out."

"Just the coffee shop."

"French Press Café? My mom was just telling me about it. I live in Chicago now, so I haven't experienced it yet. My mom's book club meets there now. Apparently, they really like the new owner."

"Really?" The man's face lit up as he cracked a smile.

He could do serious damage to a girl's heart with a face like that. Mila melted like a love-struck teenager, all shy and self-conscious. She took a step back and leaned against her car. She needed to stop staring. Besides, he wasn't going to look twice at her now that she had run him over. He probably had women from Wild Harbor flocking to his doorstep.

Mila brushed a strand of hair from her face. "I heard some guy is trying to turn the town into a year-round tourist trap."

"That's interesting." Max squinted and cocked his head,

mildly amused. "I think he's not that bad when you get to know him."

"Oh, you know him?"

"Yeah, I kinda do." He looked away, but Mila could see the corner of his mouth turned up.

"Oh, well, I'm sure he's great for the economy. I just don't want Wild Harbor to lose its small-town charm."

"Says the girl from the big city." He kept a straight face, but he wouldn't stop looking at her.

"Yeah, so? I like Wild Harbor," she taunted back.

"What makes you so invested in the town's future?"

Mila shifted her feet, unable to figure out why he cared about her answer. "I owned a bridal shop in Wild Harbor before moving to Chicago. Hardly made any money in the off-season, so my dwindling bank account forced me to close the store. I didn't want to leave. I just couldn't afford to stay." She wasn't about to unload her current financial situation on him.

"I'm sorry to hear that, but Wild Harbor has changed. Did you see the traffic on Main Street? Maybe you should reopen your shop here."

"I didn't just see it—I was stuck in it. That's how I ended up on this street. Despite the town's growth, I can't reopen my shop. There's more to the story, but it's complicated." Mila waved her hand in the air, shifting her weight. She didn't want to share her broken engagement story with a stranger. "Just know that I'm one hundred percent invested in Wild Harbor's future. My family lives here. It will always be home."

A surge of emotion bubbled up in her chest. Three generations of her Sutton ancestors had lived here. If she was being honest, part of her heart hadn't let go. But what other choice did she have? Her first shop had failed and so had her engagement. There was no way she could return and endure the humiliation of rebuilding her life again. Maybe others could stomach it, but not her. Shame ripped through her chest.

A text message dinged on Max's phone. As he pulled his phone out of his jacket, Mila noticed he wasn't wearing a wedding ring.

It was just her luck that she had hit a handsome bachelor. He'd never consider looking twice at her now that she had endangered his life. Why couldn't she have hit an *ugly* single guy? She wanted to shake her fist at the universe.

"They're wondering where I am." He recited his answer as he typed: "Hit by car. Be there soon." He glanced at her. "This will start the gossip mill."

"I'm sorry I've made you late and for the damage to your bike." Mila's gaze shifted to the bike's front tire as she kneeled and touched the damaged frame. At least it was the bike and not him. It could have been so much worse.

"Don't worry, the bike can be fixed. I'm just disappointed I'll actually have to drive the next few days."

"It will help you appreciate the lovely traffic jam that the rest of us have to endure."

"Good point." He gave her an amused grin.

"Can I drop you off at the coffee shop? Then I'll take your bike over to Joe's."

"You know Joe?"

"I got my first bike from his shop. A family friend."

Max bent over and picked up the bike like it weighed nothing. He must have some serious muscles under his riding gear.

"I'd love a ride, if it isn't too much trouble."

She reached out to take the bike. "Can I help with that? You just got hit by a car, you know." He stepped around her car like he was lifting a sheet of tissue paper. As Mila popped open her trunk, she could smell his musky scent. One part outdoors, two parts aftershave, all parts distracting.

She attempted to slide the bike into her vehicle, but struggled to angle it right. He seemed mildly amused that she was trying to assist him.

"I've got it." He put his hand out to stop her.

"But you're hurt."

"I have an abrasion on my elbow. Nothing worse than what I experienced in high school football. I'm fine, Mila, really."

She liked the way he said her name, like they were old friends, instead of a random guy she'd hit with her car.

He eyed the wedding dress in the back seat and his gaze darted to her hastily packed suitcase, which was hanging open, revealing a satin slip. His eyes glossed over the lace strap and then slid straight ahead.

"Sorry for the mess. This trip was last minute. Home for a wedding and the holidays." She pushed the slip into her bag and zipped it. "I wasn't thinking I would haul an actual person around. The only thing I transport is wedding dresses."

"Tell me about your business."

When a client stepped through her doors in Chicago, she had no problem selling five-thousand-dollar dresses. But Max had a way of making her feel jumpy, like an impostor. If she couldn't make her business work in a small town, who did she think she was trying to make it work in Chicago?

She waved it away as if her store was nothing special. "Well, it's just a wedding-dress shop." She already felt small.

"I have a feeling it's not just any wedding-dress shop."

It was the push she needed. "You want the full pitch? I sell designer wedding gowns to brides who want extraordinary dresses for their fairy-tale weddings."

"You've got a strong business tagline."

Her heart fluttered at the compliment.

"Why did you get into the industry?"

"I've always loved wedding dresses. When I was a little girl, I'd save my money to buy *Brides* magazine and pick out all the dresses I wanted to wear. Then it hit me—I'd only ever wear one dress, but I liked them all. So my fascination with dresses turned into a business after college."

"Sounds like the perfect career for you. But I still think you should reconsider Wild Harbor."

She pulled into a parking spot outside the café. Lights faintly twinkled through the frosted windows. She wondered who he was meeting and whether he was in love with her. Never mind that she didn't know a thing about him. A guy like him wouldn't be single for long.

"I appreciate the encouragement, but I'm happy in Chicago. That's my home now."

"Thanks for the ride. Maybe I'll run into you again while you're home? No pun intended."

A warmth spread across her cheeks. "If there's anything I can do to make it up to you, let me know." Too bad she had already ruined any chance she had with the handsome stranger.

"I'll keep that in mind." He turned back to wave and then disappeared inside before seeing Mila lift her hand in return.

She hadn't noticed it before, but when he walked away, it had just started to snow.

CHAPTER THREE

MAX

Max walked into the coffee shop feeling a strange pull to spin around and ask Mila if she would have coffee with him. Never mind that she almost ran him over.

His elbow throbbed from crashing into the pavement. When he'd been talking to Mila, he'd hardly noticed the pain, except for a surge of energy that pulsated through him like adrenaline. Unfortunately, Lexy didn't have the same effect, even though her laser gaze followed him through the shop like a tiger waiting to pounce.

"You're here!" Noah yelled across the shop as he frothed milk. Noah was Max's assistant at the French Press and had been working at the coffee shop since it opened. Only a few years out of college, he had boyish good looks and had become Max's most reliable employee and friend.

"What's this about getting hit by a car?" Noah scanned his body, looking for injuries. "You look like you're in one piece."

Max crossed behind the counter to grab an employee apron.

"I was crossing an intersection on my bike and never saw the car. My bike took a good hit, but I'm okay."

"Was it a tourist here for the festival? This traffic is unreal." Noah snapped a lid on a latte order.

"Actually, no. A former hometown girl named Mila. She was heading home and took a side street to avoid the traffic. It wasn't her fault, exactly. I didn't look."

"Wait. Mila Sutton? Her mom attends the book club that meets here." Noah measured out more coffee grounds. "I wondered what happened to her since her fiancé called off the wedding."

"She was engaged?" Max couldn't imagine anyone wanting to leave a beautiful woman like Mila. "Who was the guy?"

"Jake Jordan. He inherited the Beach Crest Lake House and a pile of money when his grandfather died."

"Ah, yes. We met at a town hall meeting. He made me promise to keep the winter festival as far away from his McMansion as possible—or else."

"Or else what? He'd blame you for the tourists gawking at his ostentatious beach home?"

"Or else his lawyer would call me." Max kept his back to Lexy, but he could still feel her lasers burning into the back of his skull.

Noah leaned toward Max and lowered his voice. "Speaking of people to avoid, you've got a customer waiting." He nodded toward Lexy's usual table. Max's eyes flitted over Noah's shoulder. She fiddled around on her laptop, scrolling through property listings. When her eyes caught his, she sprang from the table, ready to corner him. Nowhere to hide now.

"Hey, you're late." Lexy sauntered toward the counter. "I thought you were avoiding me."

"Just ran into a problem. What can I get you?"

"Need you ask?" She twirled a strand of auburn hair, looking coquettish. She was striking in that photoshopped kind of way, but she just wasn't the type Max fell for. A little too polished. Not the kind who stole his heart. He wouldn't repeat that mistake.

Max busied himself at the counter, cleaning up coffee grounds.

"Noah already hooked me up with my usual latte," she purred. "But he doesn't make them like you."

He wouldn't take the bait. "Noah's the best around. I'm better at business than making coffee."

"He might be the best, but there's something special when you make mine." She leaned across the counter to get his attention.

He'd rather be hit by a car than put up with her flirting. He busied himself with cleaning the espresso machine.

She persisted. "I'm assuming you'll be at the festival concert tomorrow night since you're the one who planned it. Want to meet there?" She was taking up half the counter now. Max backed away and filled a water cup, uncomfortable with the shrinking space.

"I'm helping with the festival, Lexy. It's hard to do other things."

"Then perhaps I'll see you there?" A look of expectation flickered across her face.

"Maybe." Max focused on chugging his water. A table of ladies eyed them curiously.

"Well, then, hope to see you at the concert." Her voice was like plush velvet. She slid off the counter and gave him one last flirty look over her shoulder before she returned to her seat.

He wasn't sure how to make it clear that he wasn't interested. All the hints he was sending didn't seem to get through.

Noah leaned toward him and whispered in a singsong voice, "Max and Lexy sitting in a tree—"

"No way." Max poured himself a cup of coffee. "The woman can't take a hint."

"You're not interested? She's a beautiful woman."

"Yeah, pretty, but—" He didn't quite know how to explain to Noah that looks weren't everything.

"But what, man?"

"You know how when you find the right girl, you're not interested in anyone else?"

"Uh, no. I haven't found the right one yet." Noah was just out of college, hardly interested in settling down.

"When she's not the right one, you know that, too."

"Excuse me." Someone interrupted their conversation. "I'm looking for Max."

He knew that voice. Max whipped around to see Mila on the other side of the counter. Snow dusted her hair and her cheeks were pink from the cold.

She stared at his apron as the realization swept over her. "Oh wait, it's *you*. Do you work here?"

Noah leaned into the conversation. "He doesn't just work here, he owns it."

Mila's mouth dropped open. "You mean, you're the one my mom was talking about? The guy who started the winter festival?"

"Yep." Her face was priceless, like something Max should have framed on the wall in the café. "I gotta admit it was interesting to hear what you thought about me since we hadn't even met."

She shook her head slowly. "Why didn't you tell me?"

Max was mildly amused at how cute she was when she was flustered. "You didn't seem interested in finding out whether or not it was true. I wanted to convince you I was a nice guy."

She frowned, annoyed that he'd deceived her. "If you'd been honest with me, it might have worked."

"In my defense, I had just been hit by a car, and in case you've forgotten, it was *you* who hit me. So pardon me if I decided not to embarrass you, and instead, let you off easy. Some people would have called the cops."

Her mouth dropped open slightly before she regained her composure. Her features softened like a blurred photograph. "Thank you for not calling the cops. I shouldn't have come down so hard on you."

"Maybe we should just start over?" He hadn't meant to make her feel like a piece of aluminum foil, all bent out of shape. He wanted to smooth out her curled edges.

She shifted her feet and considered. "Is there something I could do to make it up to you? So I don't become the punchline of everyone's joke?"

Max wondered why she appeared so distraught, like she expected he'd make her look stupid. "I won't spread it around, if that's what you mean."

She exhaled slowly, relief spreading across her face. "Oh, good. I know what it's like to be the talk of the town—and not in a good way."

"Oh, really?" Was this regarding her breakup? He didn't have the right to ask yet. Her guard was up like a cornered cat. "You don't have to tell me."

"You'll probably hear about it, anyway."

He didn't want to admit he already had. "I'm not here to change Wild Harbor. I want to make it a better place, where people want to stay."

"Even if the traffic is terrible, and it's bombarded with tourists?"

"I have business owners saying they've never experienced a season like this. They're thriving instead of fighting to survive. If we can save a few businesses so people can stay, it will be worth it."

The hard edges of Mila's expression disappeared. He hoped to convince her he wasn't all bad. He pushed a cup across the counter to her.

"Salted caramel latte?"

"No, really. I shouldn't."

"You should. My treat." And a peace offering.

Max rounded the counter, closing the gap between them. It was so unlike him to be this bold. "How about you give me a chance to prove I have Wild Harbor's best interest at heart?"

Mila appeared unconvinced, but the way she turned her head hinted she was listening.

"You come with me to the winter festival tomorrow, and I'll show you how this town is thriving. Plus, you owe me."

"Owe you—for what?" Doubt clouded her face.

He'd asked for too much. Max lifted his elbow to show her the gash. She lightly touched his arm, turning it over as delicately as a piece of fine china. Her fingers were like sparks across his skin.

"I feel terrible I caused that." Her face crumpled, pricked by guilt. "You should really cover it until it heals." Then she dropped his arm and stepped back, suddenly aware of how close they were.

He missed the electricity of her touch.

She wrapped her fingers around the cup. "I'm sorry for hitting you, but I rarely go out when I'm home."

"What are you, twelve?" he teased.

"No." She stood straighter, lengthening her petite frame. "I'm a homebody."

"You avoid people?"

"I don't avoid people. I'm just—"

"A hermit? A recluse?" he shot back.

"Not at all." Her eyes narrowed as she retreated to scared cat mode.

"Then come to the concert tomorrow." Max advanced closer so no one would see the energy pulsating between them. "There's a local band playing." Even as he said it, something inside him protested. This wasn't the norm. He didn't ask out strangers. "You'd be doing me a big favor. I need an excuse to get away from Lexy. I'd pay anyone to be my date just to get her off my back."

"You mean Lexy Carmichael?"

"You know her? She's the kind of girl who is—how can I say this? Persistent." He hoped he didn't sound desperate. If he could convince her to go, it would solve two problems. Keeping Lexy out and letting Mila in. A win-win.

"Sounds like she hasn't changed much." A brief, dark shadow flickered across her face as she sipped her coffee. Drops glistened in her dark hair where the snow had melted. Her expression shifted as she considered his offer. "How about this? I'll go as your date tomorrow so Lexy will get the message. Of course, we're not actually dating, but she doesn't have to know that."

Her dark eyes watched him. It was like dangling a carrot and he knew it. It's not like he had time to date anyone right now, and she wasn't staying in town for long. The offer was too good. He couldn't stop himself if he tried.

"Then I'll see you tomorrow." An energy rose in Max's chest. He felt the surge of electricity when she was near, even if he wasn't touching her.

"Sounds good. Thanks again for the coffee." She lifted the cup in a private toast.

Max watched her drift outside where the snow was falling harder, blanketing the landscape like a clean white sheet.

One date. That's it.

The last thing he needed was to get involved with a girl who was leaving town after the holidays, but he couldn't turn down this internal current of energy. He knew what it was like to be abandoned by someone he loved. So why couldn't he stop himself now?

CHAPTER FOUR

MILA

When Mila parked her car outside of Lily's home, she tried to push aside thoughts of Max. It felt like stuffing a parachute into a tiny cylindrical tube. She had agreed to be Max's date—nothing more. It wasn't an actual date, and he wasn't a real love interest.

Another idea flickered in her mind like a June bug in summer. If everything went well, perhaps he could be her date for the wedding. He wouldn't have to know about Grams's offer since he was using her as a decoy for Lexy. The fake date was the perfect solution. No pressure. No expectations. No waiting for the phone to ring or a text asking to see her again. It gave her the ideal cover until she left town after the holidays. This was so much safer than love.

The door to Lily's lake cottage swung open. "Thank you so much for coming, Mila. I really owe you for this. My sisters will be relieved to not hear me worry about my dress anymore." Lily's face held a smooth, rosy glow. It was obvious she would make a beautiful bride.

"You know it's no trouble." It was true. The Woods family had stuck by her through an awful breakup and the subsequent fallout afterward.

Cassidy edged by her sister and nearly tackled Mila. "You're finally here!" She wrapped her arms around her friend, squashing the dress she was holding.

"Careful with the gown," Mila squeaked as Cass squeezed out a lungful of breath. Cassidy didn't seem to hear her or was ignoring the request.

Oil and water were how Mila's parents described the two friends. Mila was meticulous with every detail, organized to a fault, and verged on the edge of OCD. Everything had a place. A time. A system. That's how life worked. She didn't cannonball into the pool like Cass. She only dipped her toe in.

"Let me help you." Lily lifted her dress from Mila's arms. "Mom and Megan can't wait to see you."

Cass stepped back, her long, wavy hair looking like she'd just rolled out of bed onto the cover of a magazine. Quite the opposite of Mila's carefully styled, shoulder-length hair, which was pulled back into a low ponytail and slicked down to prevent any flyaways from escaping.

Cass nearly dragged her into the living room by her elbow, where her sister, Megan, and her mom perused bridal magazines. Diane Sutton had been best friends with Becky Woods for years, and the tradition had continued when the girls were little. Cass and Mila were the same age and had bonded over fruit snacks and cheese sticks during playdates.

Mila gestured toward Lily. "Let's see the bride in her beautiful gown. Do you want help with the buttons on the back?"

The dress had an embroidered and beadwork bodice with cloth buttons up the back and a silk chiffon skirt. It was the perfect mix of vintage and contemporary, the type of dress only a distinctive bride would choose. Lily had always held an appreciation for antique things.

Lily shook her head. "Why don't you sit down and catch up with Cassidy? Megan and Mom can help."

"On it." Megan headed toward Lily's bedroom.

Becky squeezed Mila's elbow as she passed. "We're so glad you're home."

"You must be exhausted from your long day." Cassidy flopped onto Lily's sofa.

She didn't have to invite Mila to do the same. She knew the drill and sank down next to her, laying her head on the back of the couch. If she closed her eyes too long, she'd be a goner.

"I can't wait to crawl into bed tonight even if it is on a sagging mattress in my parents' home. I'll probably be asleep in five minutes."

"Really? I fall asleep on the couch most nights." Cassidy couldn't suppress a guilty smile. "I still love staying up late and watching movies."

Mila wished she could say the same, but she spent her nights doing paperwork, followed by lights out at nine. It was easy to keep this routine when you lived alone and didn't have much of a social life.

"How long are you going to be home this time? I've missed you. Can we spend time together before you bolt back to Chicago?"

She couldn't believe Cassidy even had to ask. "I wouldn't miss hanging out with you. Originally, I was planning on coming home only for the wedding. But my schedule unexpectedly changed, and I can stay until the new year."

"So that means you can enjoy the winter festival. Did you hear about the concert?"

Mila folded her hands like she was holding a little secret inside them. She couldn't believe what she was about to confess. "Yes, I have actually. I'm going with a date."

"What?" Cassidy's eyes bulged. "Who?"

"A guy I just met in town. Max Malone."

Her mouth dropped open. "The barista? How do you know him?" Cassidy was now leaning toward her.

"I ran into him on my way through town. We had a little accident between his bike and my car. Fortunately, he wasn't hurt, but it led to us chatting for a while, and now we're attending the concert together."

"Wow. That's big. Huge, actually. Max hasn't really dated anyone other than Lexy since moving to Wild Harbor. He seems committed to the bachelor life, kind of like Matt. If Lexy can't tie him down, no one can."

Mila kicked the toe of her shoe against the coffee table at the mention of Lexy. No matter how she tried to steer clear of the woman, her name kept popping up like a nasty rash.

"There's nothing between us. To be honest, he's not interested in me. It's like a marriage of convenience."

"A marriage of what?"

Mila picked the lint off her pants, afraid to meet Cassidy's glare. The idea of an arranged date sounded ridiculous. "It means we're going out for other reasons than attraction. He wants to send a hint to Lexy, but you can't tell anyone. If word leaks, then the plan will fail."

Cassidy's nose scrunched up like she just caught a whiff of something unpleasant. "It's to drive off Lexy? Why would you say yes to that? Wait—don't tell me." Cassidy shook her head.

"It's not revenge," Mila shot back in defense. At least she hoped it wasn't. "Every time I return home, people always ask if I'm dating anyone. It's like they only care about my love life. I love running my wedding shop, and I live a full, wonderful life without a man, but no one asks me about that. They can't see how a person might be happy alone." Why couldn't Cassidy understand that some women preferred a tidy existence with no attachments?

"So the arrangement is mutual? You're trying to stop people from asking about your love life?"

"Pretty much." She didn't want to mention Grams's offer to find a date for the wedding. Cassidy would balk at the idea. *An arranged date so you get Grams's money?*

It would force Mila to explain her hemorrhaging finances and the employee who had taken advantage of her kindness. How had her life become so complicated that she couldn't even confess the ugly parts to her best friend? Embarrassment burned her up like a blackened match.

Cassidy's forehead knotted into lines. "Are you sure this has nothing to do with Jake?"

Mila shifted on the couch. No doubt her feelings for Jake were mixed up in this mess. "Maybe a little, but it's not the only reason." He had scarred her in more ways than one.

Cassidy was one of the few people who'd seen the damage he had inflicted when he walked out on her wedding day.

Mila waved the thought away. "I don't want to hear about his new girlfriend."

Jake rotated through women like a revolving door. His most recent attachment was probably gorgeous with flawless skin. If Mila was going to run into him, it would be nice to not face him alone.

"To be honest, I haven't heard. But if he is, she can't be like you. He lost out big-time when he broke off your engagement."

It's not like Mila hadn't had hints that their relationship was faltering before the wedding. A month before the big day, Mila had surprised him by bringing tacos from Roberto's. But when she'd entered his kitchen, she'd caught him with a red-faced Lexy. He had passed it off as a work arrangement, but it wasn't until they broke up that Mila had put it together. His feelings for Lexy had turned into something more, but he'd been too chicken to call off the engagement until their wedding day.

Cassidy examined Mila. "Have you worked through it? The breakup, I mean."

"I've accepted it." But she hadn't forgotten it. Resentment

had grown in her heart like a bitter root. Therapy had helped and so had moving to Chicago. But it still creeped up on her in the middle of the night when she was tired. Forgiveness felt like a lost coin sunk in the bottomless ocean. Her wedding gown only served as a reminder of what she'd lost. Someday she'd get rid of it, but only after she'd finally let go.

"If you're worried that I'm still in love with Jake, I'm not. I just wish I could meet someone I like."

"Then let's find you someone." Cassidy crisscrossed her legs on the couch, the same way she had as a child.

Mila's thoughts shifted to Max. His good looks were blinding, but she knew better than to fall for a striking face. He'd at least make an interesting fake date tomorrow, if she didn't get cold feet and bail first.

Megan busted out of Lily's bedroom. "Are you girls ready to see the bride? She looks extraordinary."

Cassidy clapped. "We can't wait."

Megan peeked her head into the bedroom. "They're ready."

Mila held her breath. Lily appeared in the hall, draped in an exquisite dress that fit perfectly, like something out of a magazine. A stunning bride.

"Lil!" Cassidy jumped off the couch, meeting her sister halfway. "You look incredible. And you were worried the dress wouldn't fit?" Cassidy spun her sister around. "Hardly. It fits you like a dream."

"Whoa, careful with all that spinning. I'm still not used to these heels." Lily gave a little kick in the air, showing off the stiletto rhinestone pumps peeking out underneath. "I can't believe it either. I guess I was worried about nothing." Guilt spread across her face.

Mila joined Cassidy in admiring the bride. "It was worth it to see your face when you came out of that room. Besides, I needed some extra time at home, and your request helped me decide. I owe you for forcing me to take a break."

Becky stepped forward and touched Mila's arm. "Now, we just need to find a nice young man for you."

Of course her mom's best friend would be as interested in Mila's love life as her own mother.

"My hands are full with the shop."

"You never know how quickly things can change."

Mila wasn't about to tell her that she wanted to take her time. Find the right man. Not take any chances, which was why this fake dating thing didn't seem like a terrible idea.

It had all the perks of dating with none of the emotional ties. The perfect arrangement for someone who didn't want to fall in love.

CHAPTER FIVE

MILA

The snow continued to fall throughout the night like a winter dream, piling up on sidewalks and leaving the town blanketed under a crystal white glow. It was one reason why Mila always circled back to this town, where all four seasons were illuminated by different colors. The pastel hues of spring and lush greens of summer. The red and orange glow of fall and white sparkle of winter.

Despite the cold temperatures, a crowd still flooded the concert, bundled up in bright hats and chunky scarves. The outdoor auditorium was decked out with white lights and silver garland, turning the scene into a winter wonderland.

Mila scanned the crowd for Max and checked her phone again. Although she told herself this wasn't an actual date, her pulse raced at the anticipation of seeing him again. He made her feel things that she'd buried a long time ago, but her heart was still too bruised to entertain the thought of falling for him.

She waited in the back, trying to blend into the crowd, her

eyes flitting across the rows. The last person she wanted to run into was her ex, Jake.

A familiar voice startled her. "Hey, I almost didn't recognize you in that hat."

She spun around. Max was dressed in a navy wool coat and leather gloves. He looked like he'd stepped out of a men's magazine, the kind where men posed on snow-covered mountains.

Mila pulled her hat over her ears. "I don't like to be cold or even go outside in the winter. I'm kind of a Scrooge that way." Mila pushed her hands into her pockets. She had forgotten her gloves. *Again.*

"The hat looks good on you. I'm glad you came."

A warmth spread across her cheeks. She focused on the band setting up, hoping her red cheeks passed for frostbite. "My idea of enjoying winter is hibernating inside next to the fire."

"Well, I need to change that. Starting tonight." He held up a coffee cup. "I brought you the official holiday drink of the French Press Café, a peppermint mocha with whipped cream."

"Oh, thank you." Mila took the hot drink, and the warmth spread to her fingers. "What do I owe you? This is the second free drink you've given me."

"It's on the house. After all, you are my date tonight."

Mila liked the sound of that. She hadn't been on a date in who knows how long. She'd forgotten what it was like to be on the receiving end of someone's kindness.

She took a sip. "Wow, this is fantastic. But I'll probably never sleep tonight."

"I was hoping you like chocolate. But I'll warn you, it's addictive." His gaze dropped to her mouth. "By the way, you have a little whipped cream on your mouth." He reached up and lightly swiped the corner of her lips with his thumb.

"Oh, how embarrassing." Her face heated as his touch sent a sensation down her neck.

A worried look crossed Max's face as he muttered under his

breath, "Don't look now but trouble is coming this way." Mila turned to see Lexy making a beeline for Max. She was laser-focused on Max.

"Max, did you need a seat? I saved one in the front."

"Uh, no." Max's expression closed off like a blind being rolled down. "Unfortunately, I can't sit with you tonight. I'm here with someone." Max stepped aside so Lexy could see Mila.

Shock registered across Lexy's face and then a quick correction. "Mila Sutton?" Her tone had a note of false cheer.

"Hey, Lexy." She dug one hand into her pocket and hoped she appeared composed. If there was one thing owning a wedding shop had taught her, it was how to hide her emotions under pressure.

"I thought you moved to Chicago." It was supposed to be a jab.

"I wouldn't miss coming home to celebrate Christmas with my family." Mila steered clear of the real reason she stayed away. Humiliation knotted her stomach.

"How long are you in town?" Lexy gave her a questioning glare.

"I'm staying until the new year."

"Huh." Her brows knitted up like she was trying to figure out the situation. "Don't you love the new coffee shop? I can't stay away."

So I've heard. Mila bit her tongue. People deserved a second chance, but she wasn't sure if she could trust Lexy. Not after what had happened.

"Well, gotta run." Lexy brushed Max's arm. "Don't want to lose my front-row seats." Her eyes lingered on him before she offered a quick wave.

Max leaned into Mila's shoulder and lowered his voice. "You just saved my whole evening."

"I don't know about that." Mila watched Lexy snake through the crowd. "You're still stuck with me."

"That doesn't seem like a bad way to spend the evening." His lips quirked. "But we'll see whether the feeling is mutual."

"You're not too shabby."

"Wow. Just above shabby? That hurts." He pretended to stick a knife in his heart.

"Let me rephrase it. For a fake date, this is wonderful."

"Now we're getting somewhere. What's your history with Lexy?"

"We were good friends in high school. She always wanted to date Jake, but he brushed her off. Then a few years ago, Jake and I started seeing each other, and Lexy couldn't stand the fact I was dating him. She kept telling me he was all wrong for me. I guess I should have known."

"I'm so sorry, Mila." Max met her gaze, and there was a softness there she hadn't seen before.

An older gentleman approached Max with a wave. "You didn't tell me you had a lady friend."

"This is Mila." Max turned to her. "Do you know Dr. James? He and his wife bought a house here last year."

Mila put out her hand. "I don't, but it's so nice to meet you."

"I'm glad to see Max out having fun. He works too hard. I tell him all work and no play—"

Max held up his hand, guilty. "I know . . . it makes me dull. I'm following doctor's orders."

Mila was surprised that anyone needed to tell Max to have fun. Wasn't he out riding bikes and having adventures on the weekends?

Dr. James turned back to her. "Make sure he has fun the next few weeks, okay? He's put on a fantastic winter festival for this town, but he needs a break."

Apparently, she wasn't the only one who needed a vacation.

"Once the Christmas gala is over, I can finally call things a success. Are you coming?"

"The wife and I wouldn't miss it. She's forcing me to pull out my tux and practice our ballroom dancing. I hope you're bringing someone to dance with."

Mila's cheeks heated when Dr. James dropped the hint in front of her. He was clearly trying to force Max into asking her.

"Uh, I haven't even thought about it yet." Max shifted uncomfortably. "But we'll see."

Dr. James returned to his seat as the band started "Jingle Bell Rock." Mila sipped her coffee and glanced at the packed crowd from the back of the auditorium. As the lights danced across the stage, Mila waved at a few familiar faces from her childhood. The owner of the hardware store who had always snuck her candy. The silver-haired lady from the ice cream shop. The older couple who had greeted her at church every Sunday. They were as familiar to her as the comfort of an old blanket.

The music forced Mila to lean toward Max's ear. "You've done a great job organizing the winter festival. I can see how much the town loves it."

His breath brushed her ear. "I wish I could take credit for it. Everyone has worked to turn it into a win for the community."

It was no wonder that people loved Max. He knew how to plan a successful event. He was the type who took charge and wasn't afraid to tell people what to do.

Max motioned toward the exit. "Do you want to step outside? We can still hear the music, but can talk a little easier."

Mila followed Max down to where the hillside sloped to the harbor, their breath making cloudy puffs in the icy air. The snow had all but stopped, except for a few stray flakes that drifted from the sky like confetti. A sliver of moon lit up Max's cheekbones in a silver glow.

"Take my gloves. Your hands look cold." He pulled off his leather gloves and shoved them into her palms.

"You shouldn't have to suffer because I forgot my gloves." She tried to give them back.

"Don't even." He held up his hands in the air, refusing to take them. "Just put them on."

She liked the way he bossed her around, like she was a priority.

Mila slipped on the huge gloves. His hands were monstrous compared to hers. "Now that you know everything about me, it's your turn to be on the hot seat."

"There's a lot I don't know about you." He was trying to divert the conversation back to her.

"What led you to Wild Harbor? It's not as if this is the only beach town on Lake Michigan." Mila settled on a park bench while Christmas music serenaded them.

Max sat close to her, his warmth radiating through her coat, his elbow brushing hers.

"It was business." Max rubbed his hands together. "A friend started buying homes to flip as beach rentals. He thought this town had tons of potential, but he didn't want to live here permanently. I was working in Detroit and looking for an opportunity to invest in a place where I could put down roots. The first time I visited, it blew me away. Wild Harbor is the best-kept secret on the Michigan coast. It checks all the boxes."

"Why did you open a café first?"

"I wanted to start small and get to know people. I figured nobody would trust me if I bulldozed my way in and started making changes. My plan was to build a business from the ground up and earn people's trust first. Besides, I've always secretly wanted to be a barista."

She leaned back. "Really? You've intrigued me."

"Once I found Noah to help me run it, it freed me up to look for other investments. Since Lexy is a realtor, she got involved. Then someone asked me to be on the town's improvement district committee, and I pitched the winter festival idea. The rest is history."

"Sounds like you have a complete master plan already."

"I'm a planner by nature. But I really have Wild Harbor's best interest at heart."

He was beginning to sway her. "By best interest, you mean making money?"

"Yes and no. The town needs more stable businesses that are committed for the long haul. People who can stay longer than summer."

Whether or not Max had meant it as a jab, Mila felt a pinch of disappointment. She was another example of someone whose business hadn't made it. Never mind her personal reasons.

Max regarded her thoughtfully. "I know you don't entirely trust my motives. But I'm going to prove to you I'm Wild Harbor's biggest cheerleader. I want to see this town thrive."

A husky voice interrupted Max. The tone made Mila's skin grow cold. "Mila? Is that you?"

Mila swiveled to see her ex-fiancé standing behind her. He looked the same as the day he'd left her—black glasses and short, blond hair. Her mouth went dry. A woman Mila didn't recognize hung on his arm.

"Hi, Jake." Mila's voice cracked with tension.

"Funny seeing you here." Jake glanced at the leggy, athletic woman on his arm. "This is Scarlett. She plays beach volleyball for the Wild Harbor Wildcats."

Of course she did. It's no wonder he'd choose Scarlett. She was built like an Olympian. She had all the qualities Jake Jordan would want in a woman—perfect body, cover-model looks, a successful career. Even though she'd never go back to Jake after their breakup, seeing them together still stung.

He'd clearly moved on while she still had her wedding dress hanging in her closet. Why was it so much harder for her to get on with life when she loathed the man? She glanced back at the concert, looking for an escape.

"What are you doing here?" Mila filled in the awkward silence.

"I was about to ask you the same." His eyes flitted to Max.

"I'm home for Christmas to see my family. Oh, and this is . . ."

Jake glanced from her to Max. She hesitated, unsure of what to call Max. Her date? A friend? Some guy she hit on the road?

Max rescued her. "Hi, I'm Max." he said, putting out his hand. Jake shook it reluctantly.

"I think we've met. Aren't you the one I talked to about the winter festival traffic?"

"I am." Max didn't back down from Jake's stare.

"Seems like a good crowd. So many people in there, you can get crushed." Another attempt to deflate Max's success with the winter festival. "You two here together?"

His sudden question caught Mila off guard. They weren't together exactly, but she wasn't sure how to explain their arrangement. "Uh, you know, it's complicated."

"You can tell him." Max raised his eyebrows, his pupils dilated. He was up to some sort of mischief.

"Tell him what?"

"We're on a date." He gave her a boyish smile that nudged her to play along. He was clearly enjoying making Jake jealous.

Jake's eyes narrowed. "Really?"

Mila snuggled into Max's side. "Yes, really."

He lifted his arm and wrapped it around her shoulders. It surprised her how perfectly she fit in the curve of his elbow and how her body lit up in response. Her skin had been hungry for someone's touch, and she hadn't even realized it until now.

"Hey, man, that's great if you're on a date." Jake seemed almost too casual, like he was trying to pretend he didn't care. "It's good to see you've moved on." He studied her for a moment. Could he tell there was more to the story? He considered something. "I only want the best for you, Mila. Always have."

Mila nearly choked on her coffee. *The best?* Like leaving on our wedding day? How about the months afterward when she had to clean up the emotional destruction from his wrecking ball decision? The tension in her head was building by the second.

Max snatched Mila's hand and wrapped his firm grip around hers. A surge of energy pulsated through her arm as his thumb stroked it gently. It's like he knew she was about to go nuclear on Jake and he was padding her ego to soften the blow. "I'm glad to hear that, because I do too. I wouldn't want there to be any misunderstanding."

Jake's gaze dropped to their linked hands. "Sure. I understand. See you around." He mirrored Max's move and took Scarlett's hand as he walked away.

Mila wanted to kiss Max on the lips for saving her from embarrassment. "Well, that wasn't as bad as I thought." This date made her feel like she could face her ex without looking desperately lonely. "Did you do that for me?"

"It was the least I could do, since you did me a favor."

A smile split across her face. "Jake's face was priceless when you told him you were my date. I almost snorted coffee out my nose." Max still held her hand, and she couldn't take her mind off of it. It was addictive, like the drink he had given her. Once she took a sip, she only wanted more.

"I would like to have seen that." His mouth curved into a grin.

"There's only one problem now. What happens when he finds out we're not really dating?"

"Do you want him to think we are? Just for fun?" His eyes glittered with questions she couldn't answer.

It would be nice to let Jake think she had finally moved on.

Max considered something. "What if we could do this again? According to Dr. James, I need a date for the Christmas gala. It would be a big favor since it's right before Christmas. That way, when Lexy asks, I can say no."

"You're asking me out again?" She raised her eyebrows. If she said yes, maybe Max would go with her to the wedding. It was worth a shot.

"Yep. But only if you want to." She loved it that he never pressured her to agree.

"What do I get in return?" Mila teased.

"The satisfaction of rubbing it in Jake's face?"

"You've convinced me."

"Then it's a deal." Max gave her hand a quick squeeze. "How about a mutual agreement—all fun and no romance? After the holidays, when you head back to Chicago, we're done."

She didn't like the finality of that statement, even if it was true. A shiver ran down her body as the wind whipped through her coat.

"You're cold." He wrapped his arm around her shoulders. It had been so long since a man had touched her this way, and her body lapped it up. "Maybe we should head back to the concert?"

She wanted more of this, but there was no way she could reveal it to Max. Not now. Not ever. After Christmas, she would return to Chicago. No harm done.

He offered his hand to her. How could she say no to this?

As they walked back to the concert, he was still holding on to her, and she didn't even want to let go.

CHAPTER SIX

Max loved the smell of coffee, but today, he hardly noticed it. His mind was someplace else entirely, distracted by a different captivating scent. The jacket he had worn to the concert still smelled like Mila. Occasionally, he lifted his arm to catch a whiff. He had forgotten how intoxicating a fragrance could be. He blinked, willing himself back to common sense. Hadn't he made a promise to her? *All fun, no romance.* She had her reasons, and they didn't involve love.

But the arrangement also meant she was off-limits. That was why this fake relationship was gnawing at him. There was something innately dangerous about saying he couldn't have Mila because that made the appeal of her even greater.

The bell on the door jingled as Mila, Cassidy, Lily, and Megan entered the café and snagged the table in the front window.

"Hey, Max." Lily waved him down from across the room. "We'll be ordering soon. Just let us get settled first."

The girls were carrying an armload of bags, which they

stacked on a spare seat. They stripped off their winter coats and hats, hanging them over chairs.

Mila sat down without even a single glance his way. She pulled out a navy-blue planner that she laid on the table in front of her. Without warning, their eyes caught. She lifted her hand in the tiniest of waves and then returned to study her planner.

Was that all the acknowledgment she could give him after their date? He wanted a personal greeting. Maybe something more. He wouldn't let her get away with a wave after he had stepped in to protect her from Jake the jerk. Mila's ex deserved a punch to the face for what he'd done to her.

He filled four cups of coffee and carried them over, determined to get her attention.

Megan's eyes widened. "You know our coffee addiction well."

"You're the best, Max." Lily offered a weary look and took a cup from him.

He set a cup right next to Mila's planner. Her eyes flicked over to the coffee as she murmured a thank-you, then they slid up to him. A flicker of emotion as small as a spark lit up the flecks of copper in her irises.

At least it was an acknowledgment. But for Max, it wasn't enough. He wanted to pull her away so they could be alone.

Cassidy warmed her fingers on the cup. "The perfect treat after all the wedding errands this afternoon."

"No problem." His eyes flitted over to Mila's planner. Everything was in perfectly organized rows with lovely slanted handwriting.

"It looks like you're pretty busy." He studied the numbers as Mila tallied them.

Lily peeked over her friend's shoulder. "Mila is helping me with the final details for the wedding. But we don't have much more to do." Lily elbowed her friend. "Do we, Mila?"

Mila reluctantly lifted her eyes from her paper. "Just one

minute. I'm adding up the purchases from today. You asked me to keep you on budget."

He realized she wasn't trying to ignore him. She'd been busy taking care of details for Lily. Mila was focused to a fault, and Max took it as a challenge to get her attention.

"Hey, Max, could you bring over some blueberry muffins? I'm starving." Megan took a swig of her coffee.

"Sure, anything else?"

"No muffins for me." Lily waved her hand. "I'm getting married in less than a week, and I need my dress to fit."

Cass strained to see the case of baked goods. "I'll take the same as Meg."

"For you, Mila? Your wish is my command."

She peeled her eyes from her calculations. Her lips twitched as she hid a smile. "Tempting, but no, thank you. I'll let you know if I need anything." She gave him a look that hinted, *I'll deal with you later.*

At least he had gotten her attention.

Max went to grab some muffins from the case. As he bent over, another customer walked in, her heels clicking across the floor. He'd know that sound anywhere. *Lexy.*

Apparently, his date with Mila hadn't been enough of a hint.

He placed two muffins on a plate and tried to make his escape.

"Hey, Max." Lexy nodded toward the muffins. "It's kind of you to get me a muffin, but I don't really need two."

"They're for Megan and Cassidy."

Mila's eyes flitted toward Lexy. He had wanted her attention, but this wasn't the way he wanted to get it.

"Could I get a flat white this morning? I'm so tired from the weekend." She lifted the back of her hand to cover her overexaggerated yawn. "I have some news about the undeveloped land on the west side of town."

"Oh?" He searched a cupboard for more coffee beans. "Hang on a sec. I need to get more coffee."

"The property is still for sale if you are looking for land to develop." Lexy followed him to the storage room like a puppy, the sound of her heels an ever-present reminder that she was tailing him.

Max reached for a heavy container and pulled it down to read the label. "I'm leaning in a different direction now. I'm thinking of sticking closer to downtown and snapping up older properties that need some work rather than buying undeveloped land."

As he turned around, he nearly slammed into her. He hadn't noticed that Lexy had bridged the distance between them. She was so close, he could smell the scent of her hair.

He stumbled backward into the shelves as the container dropped out of his hands. Coffee beans skidded across the floor like marbles.

"Oh, sorry," she gushed. "I didn't know I'd scare you."

Mila appeared in the doorway, her face as placid as a pond on a summer day. The only thing that betrayed her was the tiny frantic flash across her eyes. "Sorry to bother you, but is everything all right?"

Like she could ever be a bother. Just seeing her made Max want to wrap his arms around her.

"I heard a loud crash." Mila's voice didn't betray any emotion, even though Max could tell she was shaken.

"Max dropped something." Lexy kicked a coffee bean with her foot. It skittered across the floor like a pinball. "Funny how we just keep running into each other. And always when Max is around."

Max grabbed a broom. "You're not bothering us at all. What can I get you?" He was happy to be interrupted when Lexy was around.

"Cass and Meg wondered if their muffins were ready, but it

looks like we have a mess to clean up first." Mila's eyes were wide and innocent, but her face was a static brick wall. She took the broom from his hands and brushed it across the floor.

He shifted to Lexy. "We'll have to talk about this later."

Lexy's eyes narrowed for a second, before her facial expression snapped back into place. "Don't wait too long. That land will get snatched up before you know it." Her shoes clicked across the floor as she left.

Max lowered his voice. "Brilliant timing."

Mila swept the beans into a pile. "You're welcome. But I'm not sure I did anything you couldn't have done for yourself."

"True. But as soon as you came in, everything changed." He stopped her from sweeping, his hand lightly touching hers. "I'll take care of this later. Let's get the muffins and another coffee drink for you. What sounds good?"

"Actually, you never mentioned what you drink."

She was right. His job was to sell the customer what they would prefer. He shrugged. "I'm a black coffee drinker most days."

"Plain coffee? Are you a real barista?"

Max laughed. "I am. It doesn't make sense, but I love making special drinks for other people. It's like giving them a cup of happiness."

"I wish I could make people happy with something as simple as coffee."

"I can teach you."

"Really?"

"Come here." He waved her over to the counter. "I'll teach you the Max Malone way of making coffee."

"You don't know how dangerous this is. I'm a nightmare in the kitchen. The only thing I'm good at is boiling water."

"Anyone can learn to do this. First, pour some milk in this cup."

She held the cup and glanced at the machine in front of her.

"Do you want to learn or not?" He wouldn't let her off easily.

He turned on the steaming wand while she poured milk.

"Now, just put the cup under the wand."

Mila stood back from the machine like it was going to bite her.

"You need to get closer." He took her shoulders and scooted her forward, standing so close that he could wrap his arms around her waist.

As she adjusted the wand, a violent hiccup from the steamed milk caused Mila to jerk back into him, splashing milk across her shirt.

Drops splattered across the front of her blouse as she nearly crashed into his arms. Her face heated. "See? I told you. I'm terrible in the kitchen."

Max let her lean into him and didn't move away. "You're not terrible in the kitchen. You just need practice."

He wrapped his hand around hers, then he brought the cup under the steam wand.

He had frothed milk hundreds of times, going through the motions as if he were asleep. But standing next to her, something was different as he touched her hand. Her scent. Her closeness. It was enough to turn his world from black and white into vivid color. The closeness of their bodies was like a circuit of energy lighting up everything between them.

"Are we done yet?" She peeked into the cup, her dark hair falling like curtains around her face.

The milk fluffed into a cloud of white.

"It's perfect," he assured her. But he wasn't referring to the milk.

He poured the espresso into a cup, followed by the milk, then handed it to her. "Tell me how it tastes."

She took a sip and closed her eyes. "Mm-hmm."

"That good?"

She nodded, an expression of bliss lighting up her face. "Almost as good as a cheeseburger from Brewster's."

"Have you been there since you came home?"

"Haven't had time."

"I'd love to take you tonight if you're free." He wanted to see that satisfied expression again.

A puzzled look flashed across her face. "But I thought we . . . I mean, is this part of the dating arrangement?" She swallowed, clearly unsure of his intentions.

"It doesn't have to be. I'd like to get to know you better, and I need someone who will force me to take a break from work." It was a lousy excuse, but he wanted the chance to have her to himself. "Don't you want to have a Brewster's burger while you're home?"

Mila glanced over at her friends. "Okay. You've twisted my arm. See you tonight at seven?"

"Sounds good." A small smile spread across her face as she returned to the table.

As Max watched her leave, he knew she was the type of girl he could fall for. The only problem was whether she felt the same.

CHAPTER SEVEN

MAX

Max was a stone-cold wreck when he pulled up in front of Mila's house. A pulsating beat rose in his chest like a drum, the same feeling he'd experienced when he was about to meet his date's parents in high school. Even though he'd met the Suttons before, this time was different. He was Mila's date, not just the neighborhood café owner.

The brick Colonial home was a stark contrast to his own ramshackle home from childhood—a falling-down ranch next to a scary gas station. His childhood residence looked vaguely like a scene from a horror film while hers dropped straight out of a Christmas movie. The stately red brick. Lights twinkling in the windows. A backdrop of softly falling snow. An evergreen wreath on the front door. He'd even bet her parents were the type to insist on matching Christmas pajamas for the annual holiday picture.

He was lucky if his family even took a picture. When was the last time they had all been together for Christmas? A decade or more, at least.

Max didn't plan on ever taking Mila to meet his dad. It was one topic he skirted around, avoiding any conversations about his past that revealed he was from the other side of the tracks. A single dad raising two boys on a low income only inspired pity. It helped that he had grown up over an hour away—far enough that no one knew the Malone history or the fact that they barely scraped by most weeks. No wonder his mom had left town.

Wild Harbor gave him a clean slate. He was Max 2.0, a scrappy entrepreneur building something rather than tearing it down. His family had been good at destroying things—his parents' marriage, their family, even pieces of him. But he'd let all that go, burned away like ash, leaving only a husk.

Mila's mom slowly opened the door, and a warm smile spread across her face.

"Hi, Max. Come on in."

"It's great to see you somewhere other than the coffee shop, Mrs. Sutton."

"Please, call me Diane, and you've met Brian."

All his teenage insecurities came rushing back as he tried to think of something to say. "I hadn't realized you had another daughter until we met by accident the other day."

"We heard about the bike crash." Brian shook his head. "Mila felt terrible. I'm so glad you didn't get hurt."

"It's the reason she's going out with me. Guilt." They both laughed, but Max wondered if it was true.

"We're glad Mila wants to go somewhere." Brian looked over his shoulder. "In the past, we couldn't even get her to leave the house. Even her sister, Sophie, couldn't sway her."

"Dad, what are you telling Max?" Mila skipped down the steps. She was wearing a pair of black jeans and a red sweater with a hint of firetruck-red lipstick that matched her top. The color made her skin glow. For a date at Brewster's, she was dressed to kill.

"I want you to have fun tonight. Just don't stay out too late."

Her dad wrapped an arm around her shoulders and kissed her head.

"Oh, Dad, I'm not sixteen. You don't have to vet my dates at the door."

"Honey, we're not." Diane patted Max's arm. "We already know what a great guy Max is. We won't be waiting up for you two lovebirds." She beamed at both of them.

"Max and I are just friends, Mom." Mila mouthed the word, *Sorry,* then grabbed Max's arm in an attempt to exit before her parents embarrassed her more.

"We don't expect you home early," Diane crooned. "Bye, kids!" Her head peeked around the door as she shut it.

Max had the feeling Diane was still watching from the window as they descended the front porch steps.

"You didn't know what you were stepping into when you walked in my home. My parents can be a little overbearing. They can't help themselves."

"Don't apologize. It was amusing to see you turn as red as your sweater." When Diane came into the café, she always took the time to ask Max how he was doing and if he was eating enough home-cooked food.

"I don't know if my family is normal, but my parents mean well. They've put up with so much." Mila slid into the passenger seat and ran her finger across the leather. "A Range Rover, huh? Is this what you drive when you're not riding your bike? I didn't know café owners did so well."

He laughed. "I actually got it for a great deal from a friend."

"Always wheeling and dealing, huh?"

"I jump at opportunities." An image of his father kicking a flat tire on their rusted Chevy spiraled through his mind. "Would you rather ride a bike and risk getting hit by a crazy driver?" He started the vehicle, and it sprang to life with a smooth purr.

"Uh, no, thank you." She pressed the heated seat button and sank back into the leather. "This will do just fine."

~

WHEN THEY ARRIVED at the restaurant, Max could feel the eyes of the local patrons searing into him as they snaked past multiple tables. Their appearance together would be fodder for the town's gossip mill, especially among the older couples who'd hinted to Max that he should look for a wife. He wasn't planning anything of the sort. After seeing his parents' marriage go up in flames, he was content to be single.

"No time for dating," he'd always reply. It was the way he liked things. Simple and uncomplicated.

Brewster's Restaurant was a vibrant place with the greasy food Max loved. The smoky grill scent made his stomach instantly crave a mouth-watering burger. Like it or leave it, this was who he was.

When they found a table in the back, he suddenly wished he had taken Mila to DeSoto's, the elegant waterfront five-star dining experience. She was way too classy for this joint.

"I should have asked you if there was someplace else you'd rather go." If so, he'd messed up big-time.

"Oh, no. I miss Brewster's. It has its own special kind of vibe. Their french fries with that special sauce are the best around. I could lick the plate they're so good."

He busted out laughing. "Now that's a sight I'd like to see. A grown woman finishing off every drop of sauce."

"I might be an adult, but I am not ashamed of my love for french fries. Have you had them?"

"It sounds like I need to."

"I promise they'll change your life." She was trying to make him a believer yet.

They nestled into the booth in the back corner, not too far

removed from the music and bustling conversation. It might as well have been their own private room now that they were out of eyesight. After ordering burgers, fries, and a milkshake, they settled into an awkward silence as a country singer crooned about unrequited love in the background.

"So, tonight is my chance to get to know you better—to find out what makes Mila Sutton tick." Max felt strange admitting it, although he wasn't sure why. It's not like he was making any sort of commitment to her. They were friends doing each other a favor, so why should that be weird? Maybe it was because the terms seemed unclear, a relational grey area in the midst of black-and-white attraction. No doubt she made his heart beat faster, and that put the safety of his future in jeopardy.

"Getting acquainted sounds nice after our unfortunate first run-in. Does your elbow still hurt?" She gently took his wrist and turned it over so she could see the bruise on the back of his elbow. She ran a finger over his skin like a soft feather. It had been a long time since a woman had touched him. When Lexy brushed by, he always stepped back like he was being burned by a hot poker. But his reaction to Mila was the exact opposite, like a current of electrical pulses under his skin.

The server interrupted with their drinks, and Mila released his hand. He slid a tall Christmas milkshake across the table, a sweet concoction of peppermint chip ice cream, chocolate shavings, and whipped cream topped with a cherry.

She scooped the whipped cream with her finger and closed her eyes. "You need to try this shake." She scooted the glass toward him.

He took a spoonful of ice cream. "Mmm, that is good." He hadn't had a milkshake in ages, and the sweetness transported him to childhood. "I love that you're ordering all the taboo foods. The ones girls don't feel like they should eat, so they order a salad instead."

She threw her head back and laughed. "I never order a salad

on a date. I figure if a guy can't handle my food choices now, he won't ever be able to."

He liked the sound of that. No pretense. Maybe Brewster's was the right choice after all. Under that surface of calm, there was more to Mila than he realized. "I fully approve of your choices. You seem to be a woman full of surprises. I need to learn more about you."

She took another bite of whipped cream and chocolate, loosening up with each mouthful. "I'm an open book. What do you want to know?"

"Everything."

"That's not very specific."

"Tell me about growing up here. What was it like?"

"You mean besides perfect?" She set her spoon down. "I spent all summer at the beach, learning how to swim in freezing water in May and then continuing until early October. We had bonfires on the beach when the weather turned cold. In the winter, we built snowmen and forts. We watched the lake freeze, and men bundled up like Eskimos head out for ice fishing. My dad still has this old red truck that he putters around town in, and we always bring our Christmas tree home in the back. The seasons were our way of measuring time like the tide, always returning no matter what else changed. When the weather turned bitterly cold, we turned to home and leaned on our neighbors. The people who stayed, no matter what."

"Why did you feel you had to leave?" Max almost didn't ask it, but he needed to hear the story from her. "If you don't want to talk about it, please don't—"

She shook her head. "I'm glad you asked because I'm good at avoiding the subject." She played with the spoon on the table, avoiding his eyes. "Jake and I were engaged for a year when he broke things off on our wedding day. Everyone in town showed up for the ceremony, and the pastor had to break the news. Because I owned the only wedding shop here, my clientele stopped coming in. People avoided the store. Future brides thought my bad luck would rub off on them. I was already struggling to make it in the off-season, so I started over where nobody knew my story. In so many ways, it was easier to begin again. New town. No past. But moving away cost me something."

"Mila, I'm sorry."

Mila shook her head and twirled the spoon in her hands. "In small towns, people don't forget."

Max touched her hand across the table. "You could come back here and take this town by storm. I can already see how much you care about it."

"No. Absolutely not. I can't bring my business back here when I'm still known as Jake's ex." She set her jaw.

Mila took a bit of milkshake, thinking intently for a moment. "So how much longer will you stay after you buy up all the good properties?"

Max leaned back and thought for a moment, but he already knew the answer. "I could see myself staying forever. This is the type of place where I could put down roots. Somewhere I can invest in business and raise a family. It doesn't have the glitz of the big beaches, but it has that uniquely special small-town vibe. When I started the café and designed some plans for the town, it picked up momentum as more people jumped on board. I didn't have to twist their arms. They wanted it."

"So has anyone voiced concerns?"

"Uh, yes." Max held back a smile. "*You.*"

"You've won over everyone else with your charms?"

He raised his eyebrows. "A good coffee can be very persuasive."

"Hmm. Is that why you keep giving me free drinks? Caffeine is a way to a girl's heart."

He threw his head back and chuckled. "Busted."

"Well, it's working. I can see how this place is changing."

He shook his head in disbelief. "It's crazy, Mila. Instead of people hiding out in their homes when the weather turns cold, they're seeing their neighbors in December. I've had people thanking me for revitalizing this town. So many businesses were leaving because they couldn't make it beyond the summer."

"So what happens if the economy collapses? Or another coffee shop moves in?" She was trying to poke holes at his plans.

It didn't deter him. "I stay. Hopefully, forever."

She raised her eyebrows. "Ah, so you're planning on meeting *the one* and settling down here?"

"I'm not sure about marriage," Max admitted slowly. "I prefer the company of women who hit me on the street."

She narrowed her eyes. "You've been hit before?"

"Nope. Just once. By you."

A smile spread across her face. "Thanks for making me feel special."

"And I'm not opposed to marriage, but I'm not sure it's for me. My parents got divorced when I was young. It shattered them. I vowed then I'd never let that happen to me."

Dark images flashed through Max's mind. His dad's tragic accident. The violent arguments. As a boy, he hadn't understood how much love could break you. Part of him wanted to stay as far from it as possible.

"Just because it happened to your parents doesn't mean it's going to happen to you." Mila stopped to level her gaze at him. Copper sparks in her eyes flared like gold. "There are a lot of couples out there still madly in love. That's the risk you take for love, right?"

He slowly nodded, considering it. Maybe love was worth the risk. But first, he needed more proof that not all families ended up like his.

The server interrupted with a serving tray piled with food.

"I can't wait to see you lick the special sauce off," Max joked.

She held up a fry. "Not unless you can help me eat these. Their servings get bigger every time I return."

Max snatched a handful of fries as Mila dipped a fry into sauce. For someone so petite, he wondered where she stockpiled all this food. He'd gone out on dates with women who barely ate a thing and picked at their skimpy salads all night. He liked that Mila wasn't the type to hold back.

For the rest of the night, he tried to search her body language for clues. Was she having fun? What did she think of him? Was he a complete moron for thinking their arrangement could end up as something more?

By the end of the date, he didn't have a clue. She kept her emotions hidden like a well-guarded fortress.

But one thing was becoming clear. The more time he spent with her, the more emotionally invested he was. He needed to keep his feelings out of it, but he felt like he couldn't stop himself. Every time Mila smiled or laughed, she was inviting him in, like the tiniest spark of light shimmering in the dark. He'd spent the last few years stifling this desire, but now he didn't want to resist. He was like a moth to a flame.

As he walked her up the snowy sidewalk to say goodbye, she stopped before they reached the door, a look of concern crossing her face.

"Max, I've been wanting to ask you something all night, but I've been too chicken," she admitted. "I didn't want to pressure you. But I was wondering if you'd like to—" Her voice dropped off, like she was losing her nerve.

"Yes?"

She swallowed. "Go with me to Lily's wedding? I mean, it can be a fake date . . . if you want," she stammered. "Or not." She left the answer to that question wide open.

He took her hands in his. "I like the second part of that statement. *Or not.*"

She didn't look satisfied. "Is that a yes or a no?"

"It's a yes, and let's not make it a fake date."

Visible relief flooded her face. "Thank you, Max."

He searched her face for a sign that she wanted more than a goodbye. "Wait, Mila—" Before she turned the door handle, he stepped forward to give her a quick hug. To his surprise, she nestled her head into his shoulder and melted into his arms. Her body felt right in his, like a current of energy looped between them in one continuous circle.

He rested his cheek in her hair and breathed in the scent of her hair. Had a woman ever smelled this good before? Not that he remembered. She smelled like smoky cinnamon and sweet vanilla. The same smell in his memory when he closed his eyes and made an impossible wish before he took one sweet bite of birthday cake.

"Bye, Max," she whispered before stepping inside, vanilla still lingering on his skin. He wanted to hold her longer, to inhale her smell and not forget it after a hundred years.

As he headed back to his car, his body felt as light as a balloon, like he was drifting into some unknown stratosphere where nothing could touch him.

The higher he soared, the more he wondered, *What if this isn't a temporary arrangement?*

CHAPTER EIGHT

MILA

"I have an ugly sweater for you to wear." Sophie held up a baby-blue sweater decorated with a cartoonish yeti and white fur trim ringing the collar and sleeves. It was hideous. Of course, her sister would suggest a top decorated like a cream puff.

Mila grimaced. "No, thanks." She didn't want to take part in the ugly sweater wedding shower. Call her a party pooper, but she'd be fine pulling on her usual cashmere cardigan and jeans.

"Come on, Mila. Have some fun!" Sophie threw the sweater at Mila, and it landed on her head.

Mila pulled it off, her hair sticking up from the static. "I'm not into ugly sweater parties." She held up the atrocious sweater. "Where did you get this anyway? It's horrible."

"Where do you think? Online. I wore it a few years ago to a Christmas party, and it was a huge hit. Even the yeti lights up." Sophie flipped a small switch under the sweater's hem, and the yeti twinkled like a Christmas tree.

"Ugh." Mila wrinkled her nose. "That makes it worse." She tossed the sweater onto the bed.

Sophie wasn't deterred. "At least take it with you. They may not let you into the party without it. That's how the Woods family rolls."

"Cass invited me. She's my ticket in." Mila combed through her hair with a brush and took one last look in the mirror. She wasn't a big fan of bridal showers after her breakup, but she had little choice. It was her best friend's sister, and she'd promised she would help serve food. Chopping vegetables was far more appealing than standing around awkwardly trying to make small talk.

"Will Max be there?"

Mila shrugged. "I don't know." When she'd found out the party was for both women and men, Mila had wondered if they'd invited Max, but she'd decided not to ask. She might seem too interested after inviting him to be her guest at the wedding. Not that she would mind if he was there.

Mila smoothed her hair and turned away from the mirror. "I wasn't even supposed to be around for the shower."

"If Megan and Cassidy planned it, expect some outrageous games. They're not going to let you off the hook either."

Mila cringed. "I'm only doing this because I love their family." She should have known they'd skip the fancy finger foods and formal etiquette and throw a loud, zany bash instead. It was so Cassidy.

"Take the sweater." Her sister shoved the sweater into her arms. "I have a feeling you might need it."

Mila tucked the sweater in her tote bag alongside her gift. There was no way she was wearing it.

When she arrived at the apartment, Christmas music seeped through the windows as she stepped out of her car. Cassidy opened the door, a huge grin spread across her entire face. "You came!" She grabbed Mila's arm and pulled her inside. "And you're our first guest."

"Are you surprised? I'm always first." Cassidy and Megan had decked the apartment in blinding white Christmas lights strung across every shelf. A fat Christmas tree was shoved into the corner, the top branch too tall for the ceiling. A table of gifts anchored one end of the living room while a huge buffet of finger foods stretched across the dining room table. It looked like enough food to feed a few football teams.

"How many are you expecting?" Mila was dazed by the lights and smells.

"Oh, a dozen or more. I bought too much, didn't I?" The table was overflowing with plates of food—shrimp cocktail, turkey roll ups, tiny egg rolls, and piles of desserts. Her friends would eat leftovers for a week.

Mila shrugged. "At least you won't have to worry about running out."

Cassidy frowned at Mila's outfit. "Where's your ugly sweater?"

"I didn't wear one. But Sophie made sure I brought hers, just in case. Please don't make me wear it."

"Look at me. I'm wearing a sweater that looks like it was made for a seven-year-old." Her sweater appeared to have been vomited on by Christmas unicorns. "Megan's enforcing it as a requirement for the party. You don't want to face her wrath. Seriously."

"Face whose wrath?" Megan joined her sister with a chef's knife in one hand and a stalk of celery in the other. "Hey, Mila." Her eyes swept over Mila's outfit. "Where's your ugly sweater?"

"Fine, I'll change. But if anyone else shows up dressed in their normal clothes—"

Megan waved her knife in the air. "They won't. Not on my watch."

Aspen, Megan's roommate, hurried from the kitchen

carrying a tray of food. A flashing Santa hat topped her blonde curls. "Where are the bride and groom? We can't start the party without them."

Megan checked her phone. "Lily said she's running late, but they'll be here in a couple minutes." She nodded toward a door. "Mila, you can use my bedroom to change."

Mila slipped into Megan's bedroom and quickly pulled off her sweater. Outside she could hear laughter from the street, the deep bass of a voice she recognized. She slipped her finger into the side of the blind and caught sight of Max and Matt walking up the sidewalk. That answered her question about whether Max would attend the party.

She flopped down on Megan's bed and slid the sweater over her head. A mirror on the door caught the reflection of her heated cheeks. Max's effect on her was obvious. She rubbed her cheeks vigorously, which only made the color worse, then pulled out a tube of red lip gloss, hoping that would draw attention away from her cheeks.

Why was Max complicating everything? Cassidy knew the truth about their arrangement, but no one else. How would she pull off acting casual around him when he jolted her senses like a shot of caffeine?

Mila slipped out of the bedroom and hid in the kitchen, where Cassidy untwisted the cap on a bottle of ginger ale. It made a hissing sound, like a valve releasing steam.

Mila leaned against the counter and let out a breath. "You'll be pleased to know I have on the ugly sweater, and the color washes me out. I might as well be transparent."

"You don't look washed out. Your cheeks are pink." Cassidy confirmed Mila's worst fears. There was no hiding her cheeks. "Besides, Max just showed up." She nodded toward the group of guys who had just entered the apartment. "Could you cut up some veggies? I'll be right back."

Mila's insides turned into a bundle of tangled nerves. Her pulse quickened and heat slid up her spine like steam.

She positioned herself in the corner of the kitchen, hoping she blended into the woodwork, but the blinking sweater lights made her feel like a gaudy florescent Christmas tree.

Why couldn't she squelch all these embarrassing feelings and pretend Max wasn't in the room? For once, she needed to act like a normal human being instead of a bumbling idiot. She had mastered a calm facade at her wedding shop, but Max seemed to shatter any semblance of restraint now.

She grabbed a knife and rolled a cucumber onto the cutting board. The knife sliced neat little circles.

"Hey, Mila."

She swung around, knife in hand.

"Max. You scared me." Her heart twisted in her chest. At least now she could blame her red cheeks on his surprise entrance.

Max was leaning on the island, looking adorably cute in his ugly sweater. Why couldn't he ever look bad? He could wear a potato sack and still turn heads.

His eyes flicked to the knife. "Wow. I didn't know you were armed and dangerous."

"That's what happens when you sneak up on people." So much for hiding from him. It's like he had a GPS with her location on it. "Cassidy has unofficially assigned me sous chef."

"Can I help?" He stepped next to her and pulled out a knife from the drawer. *Whap, whap whap.* He chopped celery like a professional chef on a cooking show. Why hadn't this guy been snatched up? He seemed to tick all the boxes.

As Mila reached for a pepper, she grazed his arm with her waist and a current of energy zapped her body as they awkwardly scooted away from each other.

She needed to be more careful or her face would give away his effect on her.

"Oh, perfect." Aspen interrupted, her blonde curls bouncing underneath her Santa hat. "We need the fruit and veggies out on the table. Max, be a dear and carry the fruit tray out for me, will you?"

"Sure, as soon as I finish helping the knife-wielding yeti here." A lopsided grin spread across his face as he swiped a strawberry from the fruit plate and resumed his ninja chopping session, spreading out his perfectly cut veggies and fruit like a fan. He swooped the tray onto his shoulder and handed Mila the fruit tray.

As Mila entered the living room, she recognized a few faces from school. Alex and Lily stood next to the Christmas tree, their faces glowing with light.

Megan waved her hands and stood on her toes, trying to quiet the cacophony of voices, while her boyfriend, Finn, let out a piercing whistle.

"Welcome to Lily and Alex's shower." Megan grabbed a stack of papers. "We're going to play a scavenger hunt first, so I need you to pair off."

Max turned to Mila. There was no escaping to the safety of the kitchen now.

"Should we be partners?" The way he said it, he had already decided.

"Uh, okay. But don't feel like you're stuck with me."

"Who said I was stuck?" He shrugged. "I have a feeling you're a fierce scavenger hunt competitor."

"Hmm. Guess you'll find out." She wasn't sure what he was up to, but there was a spark of something in his eyes.

Megan handed them a scavenger hunt sheet. "The rules of the game are simple. You need to find the place where each of these events or things are located and take a selfie. The pair that returns first is the winner. Watch your time and be back in thirty minutes."

Mila wasn't much of a game person, but she felt flattered

Max would choose her over one of his friends. She skimmed the list. "I'm not sure I'll be much help, though."

"Don't worry"—Max pulled on his coat—"one perk of being Alex's friend is knowing a few things about him and Lily. But let's not go in order. That's what everyone will be doing. Let's start at the bottom of the list and work backwards so we avoid running into our competitors."

"Genius idea."

He leaned over her shoulder, perusing the scavenger hunt. She could feel the warmth of his breath on her cheek, which was entirely distracting. How was she supposed to focus on a game?

Max pointed to question eight. "Here's one you might know. The location of Lily's wedding dress."

"At my parents' house. I took it home after her fitting because there was one button that was loose. I was going to fix it before the wedding. Most people will assume it's at her house and go to the wrong place."

"Then that's the perfect one to start with."

They both climbed into his car, and the engine roared to life. Neither of her parents would be home tonight, and her sister, Sophie, was having dinner with friends. That would make things easy. Sneak in and out. She wouldn't have to explain why they were paired for the game.

As they approached the house, Mila pointed down the street. "Park a few doors down. We don't want our competitors to see your car parked outside." She motioned for him to come inside. "Let's take a picture of the dress in my closet for proof."

She unlocked the door and skipped upstairs to her childhood bedroom with Max close behind her.

A wave of embarrassment washed over her as she stepped into her room. Her mom had never changed the space, and pictures from high school still papered her walls.

Max scanned the room. "It's quite the shrine to your graduation year."

"Once you get to know my mom, this will make total sense. She's got a sentimental heart."

She went to the closet and pulled out the white dress so that it hung on the door behind them.

Max held up his phone and adjusted the settings. "The lighting is terrible. You can barely see the dress because it's dark behind us. Let's move in closer." She and Max pressed into the closet door, only inches apart.

Suddenly, Mila heard a door slam, then her grandmother's voice. "Mila? Sophie? Anyone here?"

Mila dropped her voice to a whisper. "That's my grandma. Quick. We need to hide."

"But why? Is there something wrong?" Max looked confused.

Mila didn't want her grandmother to make assumptions about why they were in the bedroom. *Alone, but together.* She only had seconds to convince Max of this.

"If Grams sees me in the bedroom with a guy, she'll have a fit. It won't matter how much I explain."

"Not even if we show her the scavenger hunt?"

"No. Grandma is very formal. Proper. No boys upstairs, ever. Like, *never ever.*"

"But Thelma likes me."

"Not anymore, she won't."

Panic was rising in her gut like fizz out of a pop bottle. She shoved Max into the closet. Something like an *oof* erupted from him as she pressed in close, shutting the door behind them. In the darkness, she couldn't see a thing, but she could feel his body next to her as warmth flooded her skin.

"What are you doing?" he whispered, his breath brushing her ear. Goose bumps shot down her arms like a wildfire.

"Shhh. You don't want Grams to see you here. Believe me. She's generally a delightful lady, but she has certain ideas about what's proper and what's not." It seemed silly to be whispering, like kids playing hide-and-seek. She strained to listen.

"Then why did you bring me to your bedroom?"

"As if I could have known Grams would stop by." They had always had an open-door policy with Grams for as long as Mila could remember. It had never been a problem—until now. "If I had, I never would've asked you up here."

"It's an awkwardly tight space." Max adjusted his body, and his arm brushed her waist in the dark. Under most circumstances, this was the kind of place a person would like to be stuck with a gorgeous man. Mila lashed down the attraction inside her body, hard and tight. If her grams found her red-faced and hiding in a closet, she'd take one look and know exactly how Mila felt about Max. Every cell in her body was sending off signals.

Plus, there was the complicated issue of their dating arrangement. She hadn't explained the fake relationship to her grams, and Max had no clue about the offer of money she had made. The entire plan would fall apart if either of them knew. Her neatly organized plan was unraveling like a spool of thread.

The stairs creaked. That could only mean one thing. Grams was venturing up the stairs.

"Sophie? Mila?" Grams's voice croaked. Her bedroom door squeaked as it clicked open. Grams stepped into the room.

Max's breath brushed her ear as Mila clamped her mouth shut. His body pressed against hers and she breathed him in. He smelled like a mixture of coffee and peppermint with undertones of cedar and leather.

The heat from the closet, along with his scent, made her dizzy. She tried not to move, since the closet was filled with boxes like a carefully constructed tower of blocks. One wrong move and their hiding place would be exposed.

What would Grams do if she found them? Mila wished she had thought more about her decision to hide before she'd shoved Max inside the closet. Hiding made her look guilty, but she had panicked and done the first thing that came to mind.

The door clicked shut as Thelma continued down the hall. Finally, Thelma's footsteps retreated, descending the steps.

"Do you think—" Max whispered.

Mila couldn't see his face, but she turned her head away. "Not yet."

Then the front door squeaked open and thudded shut.

Mila let the air out of her lungs in a slow exhale. Her fingers trembled as she blindly reached for the door handle, touching Max's fingers at the same moment.

"I think we're safe." She nudged the door open. He pulled on her arm to stay.

"You were always safe with me."

She nearly stumbled out of the closet. "Yes, but I'm sorry about shoving you in there."

Max stepped out reluctantly, blinking against the light. She had the feeling he had enjoyed hiding in there. He smoothed his rumpled shirt and ran his hand through his hair. "That was interesting. What would you have done if Thelma had opened the door?"

"It wasn't my smartest moment. I had no plan B."

"Nothing? How about an official introduction?"

"What would I call you? A friend? My date?"

"Just Max."

"Ha, ha." Her tone was laced with sarcasm as she swatted his arm. "I would have introduced you as my friend. Is that good enough?"

"I don't know, is it?" He let the question dangle in the air.

She clamped her mouth shut. She wasn't about to answer.

He smoothed a tendril of her hair. She could only imagine how distraught she must appear. The sweat still clung to her back.

A softness threaded through his voice. "When in doubt, confessing the truth always makes for a good plan B."

But the truth was becoming hazy for Mila. Was Max just a convenient solution, or someone she could really fall for? Was her grandmother's money the only thing that mattered in this game? She should tell him now. Call it quits before she got in too deep. She'd find a way to keep her wedding shop afloat without Grams's money.

"Max?"

"Yeah?" He was patting his pockets, looking around the room.

"I need to tell you something."

"Okay, but hold that thought." He held up a finger, still distracted. "I dropped my phone somewhere when you shoved me in the closet."

He bent over on hands and knees in the closet. "Would you mind helping me search? We're never going to finish the scavenger hunt at this rate."

"Sure. No problem." It figured that now she was finally brave enough to confess, and he wasn't paying attention to her.

"I found it!" He backed out of the closet, phone in hand, like he'd discovered buried treasure. "It had fallen between two shoeboxes. Good thing that didn't go off while Thelma was in the room." He checked the time on his phone. "We've lost a lot of time. The scavenger hunt is ending in five minutes."

"It's my fault. I'm sorry."

"Hey, no need to apologize. It's just a game, right?"

Just a game. But Mila wasn't talking about the scavenger hunt anymore. It was the apology she knew he deserved, but couldn't say. She hated how hard it was to admit the truth.

"You look upset." Max took the scavenger hunt paper from her hands. "Like winning this was something important."

He left her bedroom, but she remained behind, his scent still lingering from when they had been crushed together in the closet.

Had she learned nothing at all?

This wasn't supposed to be a game where they both lost, but she was beginning to think there was no other way.

THE REST of the shower was a blur of games, food, and bodies in a cramped space. Matt and Aspen won the scavenger hunt, and no one seemed to notice that Max and Mila returned late, the scavenger hunt sheet neatly tucked away in Mila's purse. The picture they had taken would be a reminder of a snapshot in time, a quick decision to hide instead of face the truth.

A wedding bingo game was forced upon guests next, followed by a trivia game about the bride and groom and a flurry of present unwrapping.

Mila blended into the background, refilling empty trays of food, lining up peppers in a meticulous row of green and red. She debated whether she should pull Max aside and tell him about her grandmother's offer. It was the right thing to do, and he could make his own decision about whether to accompany her to the wedding. But there was something holding her back, a tiny fluttering in her stomach that she was afraid to let loose.

With every moment they spent together, the fluttering strengthened, and so did the desire to keep Grams's offer a secret. She didn't want to ruin their relationship when it was still fragile, or for him to believe she'd used him to save her business. But now everything was changing, and she couldn't figure out how to convince Max of her feelings and prop up her hemorrhaging financial situation.

Max tipped his fingers to her from across the room. He had gotten stuck in the corner of the apartment during the gift unwrapping, wedged between a potted plant and some guests sitting in folding chairs. He leaned against a windowsill, his sweater outlining the sharp lines of his body. Mila tried not to watch him, but it was impossible. They were like two magnets, polar opposites pulling toward each other.

Max slid his eyes her way, and his face softened. It wasn't exactly a smile, more like a secret hidden under an amused expression. He lifted his punch cup like he was toasting her in a silent acknowledgment. There was no way he'd make it out of that corner until the shower was over.

As soon as the gifts clogged the floor and a trash bag bulged with torn wrapping paper, the crowd disbanded. Guests folded chairs as people searched for winter coats and missing gloves that had been piled on beds.

The snow was falling again. Mila could see it sticking to the edge of the window, a thin layer of white covering the brick, stretching like a soft blanket across the street. As Mila cleaned up leftovers, Max pinwheeled across the apartment, snatching stray punch cups as he approached. When he finally made it to the kitchen, he had a half dozen stacked like a tower of blocks.

"How many more do you think I could get on here?" He held the stack up, proud of his balancing achievement.

"Don't press your luck," she shouted over the crowd as she washed an empty tray.

The kitchen was a galley design, long and narrow with cupboards on either side. It wasn't designed for a crowd, two at most, and even then, it was an intimate space. As she took his cups from him, she noticed the closeness of their bodies, surrounded by half-eaten cheesecakes and demolished trays of fruit. She missed her clean, uncluttered countertops in Chicago and her space to breathe. Max opened the fridge and started stacking the leftovers inside. With his head buried inside the door, he took a container of strawberries from her hands, their fingers touching for the briefest second, the shock of it like sparks between them.

"Tomorrow night, the new outdoor ice-skating rink is opening. I wondered if you wanted to go with me."

Mila handed him a container of blueberries. "Does this mean I have to skate?"

"You'd be my ice-skating partner, but I promise, no Olympic lifts."

"You haven't seen me skate yet. You might reconsider."

"I won't force you to skate." He closed the fridge door. "It's a grand opening for the community, followed by the tree lighting in the park. You'd be doing me a favor."

A favor. Like a personal transaction. It's what he had said about their first date.

She turned on the water and squeezed a drop of blue soap into it. The bubbles immediately blossomed into a cascade of white. Mila scrubbed a plate, avoiding his question, focusing on the blueberry juice as it drained into the sink water. His ask was part of the agreement. For once, she wished it wasn't.

"You don't have to go, but I'd love it if you did." He pushed up his sleeve, and she could see the cords and muscles in his forearms like a map she wanted to trace. He took the plate from her and wiped it with a towel, then he opened the cupboard door and stacked the plate inside. His arm brushed her shoulder. Then he threw the dish towel over his shoulder and held his hands out for the next plate. She wanted to place her own hands in his, to know what it was like to have her palms stroked by his perfectly long and delicate fingers, like a pianist's. The pads of his fingertips would sweep over every nerve in her hand, making music only she could hear in her mind.

"I'll go." She handed him the wet plate. He circled the plate with the towel, stacked it in the cupboard, and threw the towel over his shoulder again. They fell into a rhythm of washing together. Wash, hand, circle, stack, towel. They were in sync, like musicians playing to the beat.

He reached for another plate. "Am I asking for too much?"

She shook her head, handing him another plate. "It's not too much." The fluttering in her stomach pulsated again, a tiny butterfly vibrating against the enclosure of her ribs.

She pressed her abdomen against the counter, hoping to squelch the feeling. Nobody, since Jake, had made her feel this way.

"Are you sure?" He swiveled toward her, and she could feel his eyes boring into her. If she looked at him now, he might read her thoughts and see that the fluttering wasn't nerves, but a spell he had cast on her.

"I'm sure." She circled the plate with her soapy rag, then rinsed it.

"I'll pick you up at seven." He dried and stacked.

She turned her face away, hiding a tiny smile, pretending the fluttering hadn't just swelled inside her. It was the same feeling when music moved her, the swell of a symphony rising like bubbles to the surface. She could almost laugh, but instead, she kept her face down, watching the foamy soap slip off the plate and catch on her fingers. She knew her happiness was as fleeting as these bubbles, but she wanted it anyway.

CHAPTER NINE

As Mila adjusted her hat in the mirror, Sophie came around the corner and leaned against the doorframe.

"I can't believe you're going out again." She squinted her eyes, trying to read Mila's mind.

"What's wrong with that?" Mila avoided her sister's gaze.

"You usually hunker down by the fireplace and don't leave the house until you're headed back. Max must be a pretty special guy."

"He's nice," Mila said blandly as she finished securing her earrings. She didn't want her sister to suspect anything. "We're just friends."

A twinge of guilt twisted her stomach. Trying to pretend there was nothing between her and Max was becoming more difficult by the day.

Sophie wasn't deterred. She crossed her arms and tilted her head. "Just friends, huh? You started out opposed to him and his plans for the town. I don't get it, Mila."

"I don't really have an explanation. He's been nothing but a gentleman. I just don't see a future for us." Mila stopped fussing with her hair to look at her sister. "I've got my shop in Chicago and he's set on living the bachelor life. Neither of us is interested in anything long term."

"Maybe he'll change your mind, or you'll change his."

"I'm not interested in changing anyone's mind. What's wrong with going out with someone for fun?"

Her sister shook her head. "Nothing at all. I just thought—" Sophie considered something.

"Thought what?"

"Never mind." Sophie waved her hand. "Not important."

"It is, or you wouldn't have brought it up." She turned from the mirror to face Sophie.

"You told me once you were tired of playing games, and you'd never go out with someone unless you could imagine a future with them."

Her sister was right, of course. But there was too much at stake now. Her business. Her heart. All of it.

Mila shrugged. "Maybe I've changed." Then she walked out of the room.

Max picked her up fifteen minutes early with a gingerbread latte in hand.

"Wow, you really know the way to a woman's heart." Mila picked up the hot drink and breathed in the scent. Notes of ginger and cinnamon with a hint of brown sugar. These scents were becoming inextricably tied to Max, imprinted on her memory so that she'd never be able to smell coffee again without thinking of him.

"Tell me if you think it has too much cinnamon." Max opened the door of the car for her. "Noah and I have differing opinions on how to make it."

"It's perfect." She climbed inside, closing her eyes and letting the warm smell of gingerbread envelop her. Lakeview Drive glowed with lights as they headed toward the ice-skating rink.

"I have a confession." Mila had to warn him before they reached the rink. "I'm a terrible skater. You might not want to be seen with me by the end of the night."

"Are you kidding me? I can't wait to skate with you."

"If you aren't laughing at my clumsiness."

"I promise I won't. And I'll take out anyone who does."

No wonder the ladies in the book club couldn't stop gushing over him.

A bald man, dressed in a classic long overcoat, approached them when they arrived at the rink. Mila recognized him immediately as Brad Williamson, Wild Harbor's new mayor. After the scandal with the last mayor, Brad had stepped in to take over the town's affairs. He was professional and courteous, and—unlike the last mayor—didn't seem to be in it for the power or connections.

"Max, I'm glad you came. We were just talking about you. Would you like to do the honors of cutting the ribbon after I welcome everyone?" Brad offered Max a pair of scissors.

"Isn't this your job?"

He waved it away. "I get to cut ribbons all the time." The mayor pressed the scissors into Max's hand. "You're the one who helped make the rink happen. I'm glad you changed your mind about attending." He slapped Max on the back and then shifted his attention to Mila. "We owe you for getting him to the rink's grand opening. I don't know what you did to twist his arm, but thank you."

Mila shook her head. "Oh, I had nothing to do with Max attending."

"That's not what I heard." He gave her a knowing look before his assistant interrupted them.

"What did he mean by that?" Mila whispered to Max.

"You know how gossip spreads in this town. They'll have us pegged to be married before the night is over."

She pulled on his elbow to stop him. "Is it true you weren't going to come tonight?"

Max edged away from the crowd. "Partially. Lexy had been pressuring me to come with her. But now that you're here, I don't have to worry about it." Max wrapped his arm around her shoulder.

Since their date at the concert, she had tried to forget the reason Max had first asked her out. But his offhand comment made her feel like little more than a prop, a PR stunt meant to take off the pressure of being Wild Harbor's most eligible bachelor.

Several older women stared at Mila as they made their way to the front of the crowd. *Lucky girl,* they seemed to say. In a few weeks, she would head back to Chicago, leaving behind Wild Harbor and her feelings for Max. Was she really that lucky?

He leaned close to her. "Do you want to help me cut the ribbon? I'd love to have you by my side."

She didn't want to stand in front of everyone and give the impression they were a couple. "Do you really think it's a good idea? I didn't have anything to do with this."

"Except you're the reason I came tonight. Please?" When he begged, her resolve melted. Every time.

"If you want me to."

He held out his hand, and Mila grasped it, entwining her fingers through his. The warmth of his palm radiated into hers as he led her up the steps. If holding hands always felt this good, she'd never let go.

The mayor welcomed the crowd with a huge smile, then nodded toward Max. "Would you do the honors of opening the Wild Harbor ice-skating rink?"

"I'd be honored." Max gave her hand a quick squeeze and cut the ribbon with one quick motion. As he turned his back to the crowd, he winked at Mila, spinning her heart in circles like a car on ice.

As the ribbon fell to their feet and the crowd cheered, Mila witnessed the pride on his face. If there were any doubts about how the townspeople felt about Max, he'd certainly erased them. Max was Wild Harbor's darling.

He held out his hand again. "Would you do me the honor of having your first skate with me?"

"As long as you'll catch me when I embarrass myself." Mila placed her hand in his.

"You have nothing to worry about." His smile erased the nagging questions in the back of her mind about what would happen after the holidays. She didn't have to figure it out now.

After sliding on their skates, Max took off for a quick lap around the rink before Mila even made it a few feet. As she wobbled across the ice, Max pulled up in a sharp stop that she'd only seen hockey players pull off.

"This may have been a bad idea." Her hands gripped the railing. "I'm going to end up in the emergency room tonight."

"Not if I can help it." He offered his arm to her. "Let me assist."

She inched away from the railing and clutched his elbow, trying not to pitch forward face-first.

"Whoa, slow down there." Max held her arm steady. "Maybe I should skate in front of you."

"So you can see me fall? I'm not sure that's going to help."

"Let me try." He flipped his body around and skated backwards, gripping both of her hands so he could steady her balance. Skating face-to-face meant she could get lost in his sea gaze. He was casting a spell, and her mind whirled with the nervous energy of his closeness.

"I didn't know you could skate backwards, too. Is there anything you can't do?"

"Lots of things. I just haven't told you about them yet. Now if you want to learn to skate, you've got to trust me. Don't push away. Just let me pull you along until you learn to find your legs."

As he led her in an awkward skating-dance, she felt the tension of his gaze locked on hers. Depending on the light, his irises changed from steel grey to peacock blue—an ocean so deep she wanted to swim in them.

"I'm pretty sure you're doing all the work." Not that she minded. He was the only reason she hadn't fallen yet.

"Let's see if you can balance on your own." He released her hands, and momentum pulled her forward for a few steps before she lost her balance and stumbled forward into his arms. Tangled in his coat, she found herself in an awkward embrace.

"I've got you." He held her for a moment before she stood upright. She wondered if he enjoyed the closeness as much as she did. When she finally took a step back, he seemed reluctant to let her go.

"You're not quite ready to skate on your own. Take my hands. We'll go around for another lap."

Snow drifted in big flakes. Mila could feel them landing on her face and saw them slowly gathering on Max's hat. Together they completed a lap, then two, but Max didn't let her go. He didn't seem to want to. If Mila was truthful, she didn't want him to either. She could skate this way all night.

"When the rink idea was proposed, I thought only the kids would like it." Max guided her around a boy who had taken a spill on the rink. "But I'm having a good time, and I don't think I'm the only one."

Mila noticed several couples had joined them, skating in their own world, oblivious to everything but the person they were with.

She tried not to think ahead to the days after Christmas, when this would all disappear, just like Cinderella at the stroke of midnight.

"I'd love to get to know your family more." He brought it up like he'd been thinking about it.

Under normal dating circumstances, she'd be thrilled. But she was already afraid her parents might get too attached to Max. Her breakup with Jake had made her protective of their hearts.

"I'm sure they'd feel the same." Something in her softly protested. "As long as we don't get their hopes up. When this is over, and I head back to Chicago, I'm worried about how much it's going to hurt them."

Max slowed his skating. "I wouldn't hurt your parents or you."

"Not on purpose. I don't want to give my parents an impression of something that isn't real."

"You think I wouldn't be real with your parents?" He furrowed his eyebrows, hurt by her claim.

"My parents already adore you. But I can't have you pretending there's something between us if it's temporary. You need to be honest. Let your guard down."

"What if I already have?" He stopped on the rink in front of her, forcing her to halt abruptly.

"What?" She shook her head, not understanding. She was unusually close to him now, near enough for him to lean in and kiss her. She couldn't go there. Not in front of all these people.

"What if I'm not pretending?" He zeroed in on her with an intensity she hadn't observed before.

Mila narrowed her eyes, unable to respond, when somebody crashed into her. The impact caused her to slam into Max, knocking him over and taking Mila with him. They landed in a heap on the ground with Max's arms around her, protecting her from the impact of the fall. Mila lifted her head and blinked.

A child had lost control and collided with them. He quickly hopped on his skates with an apology before racing away like nothing had happened.

Mila bursted out laughing. "I think that kid has a career in hockey. Are you okay?"

"I'll know when I stand up. But I kind of like the view." She was perched on his chest, tangled up in him. Their crash was the kind of train wreck no one could look away from.

Mila wanted to rewind their conversation and understand what he'd meant about letting his guard down, but the moment had been ruined. At first, their chemistry had just been harmless flirting, but now her emotions swirled in confusion. This was more than chemistry. She was starting to really fall for him.

The heat crawled up Mila's neck as she climbed off and sat back on the ice. "I'm fine." She avoided looking at him, wiping her hands on her pants as her body released the numbing shock of the fall.

Max handed her a glove that had fallen off. "If that's what it takes to get you closer, I'd gladly do it again." He gave her an amused look before slowly standing.

Her knees wobbled as he helped her back on her feet, and a pain shot up her arm. Apparently, she had landed on her wrist funny when she'd fallen. She winced as she moved her fingers.

"Are you hurt?" Max touched her arm.

"My wrist and my pride."

Max helped her over to a bench. "Let me see it." He gently took her hand in his and turned it slightly.

"Ow. That hurts."

His brow furrowed. "I think we should get some ice on it."

"There's plenty of ice here." She gave him a wry smile. "I could just lie down on it."

"Given our luck with accidents tonight, I think my apartment is safer. I have some ice packs there. Why don't we head over?"

They drove to Max's second-floor condominium in a brand-new, high-end complex. As he flipped on the lights, she could see he had immaculate taste. Quartz countertops. Luxurious but understated leather furniture. Shiny wood floors, and the consummate detail of every bachelor pad: a gigantic flat-screen TV mounted on the wall. Every detail was smooth, modern, and glowing. It looked like a model home that no one lived in.

"I wasn't expecting this. Your place is amazing." His attention to detail permeated every surface.

"So you thought I lived in a pigsty?" he teased.

"It's so shiny and clean, like a commercial." She ran a finger over the smooth island countertop.

"I don't spend much time here, and no one lives with me." He plucked an ice pack out of the freezer.

"That's a shame." She sank into the leather couch and rubbed her hand across it, smooth as butter. "I assumed you lived in one of your investment properties."

"None of them were ready. When I saw this new condo, I couldn't resist."

Max settled next to her and pressed the ice pack to her wrist.

She winced. "That's painful." If the cold wasn't so distracting, she'd enjoy this awkward handholding. She wrenched her wrist away.

He grabbed it back, intent on numbing the pain. "I know it hurts, but give it a minute. It gets better."

She scanned the room and noticed the empty mantel above the gas fireplace. "It's surprising to see that the founder of the winter festival doesn't have a single decoration up. Not even a tree. Are you afraid to mess up your apartment?"

"I'm not that much of a neat freak. It's not that much fun to decorate when there's no one to see it. With my work schedule, I'm hardly here. It feels pointless to put up a tree for myself."

"You didn't expect me to pop in for an impromptu visit?"

Max stretched out, his body elongating and softening. She wanted to nestle into his side and let her head sink into the curve of his shoulder.

Max leaned his head back. "I thought you wouldn't want to come over."

"Really? Why not?"

"So far, everything we have planned together has been around an event. It's safe that way. Letting someone into your home is totally different. They finally see the normal details of your life."

"I showed you my closet," she countered. "So we're not even until I see yours."

"You shoved me into your closet, only because you had to." He readjusted the ice on her wrist, considering something. "But if you want to see my closet, be my guest. Snoop around the place. I can guarantee Thelma won't be coming here, and you know you want to."

Her grams would only be too delighted to snoop around Max's place. She was undeniably nosy.

"Oh, I couldn't possibly." She shook her head. "I can't poke around in your personal space. It feels wrong." Seeing his home was another level of intimacy.

"Why is it wrong?" He cocked his head. "If I'm going to the wedding with you, we should probably be more than strangers."

The mention of the wedding jolted her back to the conversation she needed to have with him. Grams's offer. The money she needed to save her store. The words felt muddy and stuck in her throat. She cared too much about what he thought of her now. "Grams was pressuring me to find a wedding date, and you're doing me a huge favor. Kind of like Lexy."

He took her hand and delicately turned it over so he could examine her wrist. His fingers lightly flitted across the swelling. His eyebrows knitted. "Avoiding Lexy was initially a good excuse, but that wasn't the real reason. From the moment we met, I wanted to get to know you."

"When I ran into you?"

"When you stood over me after the collision, I thought maybe I'd died, you were so beautiful."

She gave him a playful smack on the arm with her good hand. "You didn't. You're making this up." She couldn't stand him teasing her this way.

He lifted his hands in mock surrender. "I'm not. I promise. You were like a vision, and I thought, *A beautiful woman has run me over. It's my lucky day.* Then I felt the pain and knew I wasn't dead."

The imaginary butterfly fluttered against her rib cage from his compliment. His hand went back to lightly stroking her wrist. It felt so soothing she almost couldn't feel the pain anymore. She wanted to melt into a puddle on the floor. He was dissolving her with his words.

"You did not think that. You're lying." She was terrible at accepting compliments. Maybe it was because Jake had broken her down for good.

"Why would I lie? You're beautiful. I bet you get told that all the time."

"Oh, no, not really." She hadn't had a date in a long time. The last time she'd heard those words had been on her wedding day, before everything had fallen apart. Something painful twisted inside her.

He searched her face. "After these last few dates, going out with you doesn't feel the same anymore."

"What do you mean?"

"I don't have to pretend. Being with you is a natural fit. Like chocolate and coffee."

Mila shook her head. "But this"—she motioned to them—"is temporary. I was your fake date. A decoy."

"First date, yes. But not anymore. This time, I don't want to pretend."

"What about the agreement—the *all fun, no romance* part?" A panicky feeling was gurgling up her center.

He frowned. "Is the idea of dating me totally repulsive to you?"

"No, not at all. Quite the opposite, actually." The words tumbled out of her before she could even stop them.

She couldn't admit her feelings now, not when she had been planning on telling Max the truth. He'd just foiled her plans by laying out his feelings. No matter how she explained it, asking him to the wedding made her look like she was using him for her own gain. There was no way he'd believe she felt something for him now.

She pulled her hand away and wrapped the ice pack around her wrist tightly. The ice stung as the pain drilled up her arm.

He squinted, trying to read her thoughts. "I've scared you by confessing all this. You'd rather be friends. Not emotionally invested."

"Um, no, that's not it at all." Why did she have to sound so dumb? Her throat felt constricted, like the words were lodged in it.

She rubbed her hand across her face. "I do want to date. You, I mean. But . . ." Why couldn't she put her words together like a normal human being? She'd lost her mind. Worst of all, she couldn't seem to focus enough to complete a coherent sentence. Her wrist throbbed painfully, and she was flustered. "I have obligations."

"To what?"

"My store in Chicago. My coworker who is covering until the holidays are over. I have another life, and it's not here."

"That's an easy fix. Come home on weekends. I'd hire you at the French Press in a second." His mouth quirked, trying to lighten her mood, but she wouldn't crack.

Her objections were floating around her head like annoying little gnats. She wanted to swat them away. "I don't see how this —us—could work. I can't let my family think there's something to hope for."

"Why not *try*?"

"Because you don't really know me."

"Isn't that what dating is for?"

"Yes, but . . ." The words faded as quickly as a firefly's glow. It wasn't just confessing the truth about Grams's offer. She feared getting hurt, of putting her heart out and being rejected, just like she had with Jake. That was the terrifying truth she couldn't name.

Max searched her face. "I think you're afraid to fail."

How could he see right through her? It's like her skin was transparent, a thin veil over her heart. If he could see her fear, then he could see everything she felt for him.

"Don't you even—" she said, pointing at him. "I've failed, Max, in so many ways. Business. Relationships. It's why I can't let myself get mixed up with falling in love."

An intensity seeped into his face. "Then stop putting up walls."

"I don't know how."

Before she could finish answering, he reached for her, his pupils wide and black. His face moved close to hers, their foreheads touching. His eyelashes lowered to a half-moon shadow, and she felt herself being pulled into his arms before his soft lips met hers. He kissed her gently, almost like a whisper, a soft invitation to stay.

He tasted sweet, like a long, slow sip of a hot mocha. His kiss only made her want more of him. Her breath came in short, tight bursts. She wanted to push him away. She wanted to stay. Her emotions crackled like electricity, lighting up with a delightful but irritating glow. He had so much power over her. He had no idea. She wrenched away and stumbled to her feet, afraid he'd see the longing in her eyes.

"Max, what are you doing? Flirting. Kissing me. I'm leaving after the holidays."

"I'm not asking for any kind of agreement. We can spend

time together while you're here. Don't race ahead to the future. Just don't run out on me."

"I need to go." Anger laced through her words. "Get my head cleared."

"Listen, I'm sorry. I thought you felt the same. The signals you were sending me—I assumed too much. Don't leave this way." He stood there, looking as helpless as a lost animal, trying to stand between her and the door, blocking her from leaving. "Besides, you can't walk home from here. Let me take you."

"Please don't. The walk will clear my head." She stepped around him, intent on leaving.

"Mila, please—" He grabbed her arm, and his touch lit her up. She needed to get away before it burned her for good.

"I can't stay." She wrenched her arm free. The glow inside her dissolved.

She knew if she stayed, she wouldn't be able to keep up the walls she had carefully built to protect herself. The ones that kept her heart hidden, safely tucked away from ever being hurt again.

CHAPTER TEN

The next morning, Max woke up with two things on his mind: apologizing to Mila and coffee cake. The French Press Café's famous blueberry Christmas coffee cake was being delivered to the shop this morning by Charlotte St. James, who made ridiculously decadent baked goods in town.

He'd make a quick trip over to the shop, pick up the coffee cake, and surprise Mila with it. If the breakfast treat didn't make her forgive him, then nothing would. He grabbed his phone and sent her a quick message.

Max: I'm sorry about last night. Please forgive me. You're beautiful, and I have no expectations for you to date me. I promise. P.S. How does coffee cake sound?

After checking in with his coworker, he grabbed a cake box and headed to her parents' home. Usually, he worked in the mornings because making the café a success had been his top priority since he opened it. But his life had been shaken up in a good way ever since Mila had entered it. Work could wait.

He rang her doorbell, and a stony silence followed. As he waited in the dim morning light, he realized that he'd never heard a response from Mila.

The lock on the door clicked open. Diane's face registered surprise, then a smile as she opened the door. "Max, this is a pleasant surprise. Please come in." Judging from her reaction, his visit was entirely unexpected.

"Good morning. I'm guessing Mila never got my message. I brought over some of Charlotte's Christmas coffee cake for the family."

"As far as I know, she's still asleep. But I'll wake her." Diane stepped onto the stairs.

"Please don't. I should have called first." He was intruding. She might order him to leave if she knew what had happened between them.

"No, it's no trouble at all." She motioned for him to follow her up the steps. "I wouldn't want you to walk into the wrong room."

He wasn't about to confess that this wasn't the first time he'd been in her room. He only hoped Mila wouldn't kill him for coming so early. One look at his watch revealed what he suspected. It wasn't even seven o'clock yet.

Diane knocked gently on Mila's door. "Sweetie, can I come in?"

There was a pause, then a muffled, croaky voice. "It's too early."

Diane turned to Max. "Wait here for a second."

She opened the door, just wide enough to squeeze through.

"Honey, Max is here, and he brought you something."

"What? Did you say something about Max?" A strange alertness colored her tone.

"He brought breakfast, so I invited him in."

"Wait, what? He's here now?" He could hear Mila's voice rise with surprise.

"Yes, right outside the door." Diane swung the door open.

Mila sat in her bed, her covers pulled to her neck. Her mother was smiling, obviously pleased with revealing the surprise.

"Mom! I'm not even presentable!" Mila tried to smooth her hair, which was rumpled and sticking out in several directions.

Diane leaned forward to Max. "Come down when you're ready to eat." She strode off, leaving them alone. Apparently, she didn't have the same feelings that Grams did.

"So, this is embarrassing." Mila frowned.

"I didn't mean to surprise you like this. By the way, what about the *no boys in the bedroom* rule?"

"My mom isn't worried about you when I look like this." She swept her hand over her tousled hair, which looked like she had rolled all over her bed. Not that Max was going to tell her that. Her raccoon eyes gave away the fact she had slept in her makeup. She looked ridiculous and enticing at the same time.

"I wanted to bring over coffee cake as a peace treaty. I wasn't intending to stay." He sat on the edge of her bed and handed her the box.

"Did you expect me to eat all of this?" Her eyes widened.

"It's for your whole family. I figure I can still get on their good side, even if I'm not on yours." She still had the covers of her comforter pulled up around her like armor.

"My mom doesn't know a stranger, Max. She'd invite the mailman into our house without hesitation." She smoothed her hair around one shoulder. "Sorry if I'm a little scary looking."

"You're actually pretty cute. Even with your hair sticking out."

She stuck her tongue out at him, and he saw a younger, more carefree version of the girl who prided herself on appearing put together at all times.

"Well, you have to stay now. My mom won't let you leave until you've eaten some eggs and bacon with the coffee cake. But don't think I'm letting you off the hook for last night."

"I was hoping you'd let me apologize. I pressured you into making a decision, and the entire night went terribly wrong. Please forgive me."

Something flashed across Mila's face like she wanted to say something, but was struggling to find the words.

Max touched her hand. "Can I see you while you're still here? No expectations. No pressure. I promise."

A sleepy smile stretched across her face. "I'd like that. Let me get dressed, and then I'll join you downstairs." She nudged him off her bed, then grabbed his elbow before he scooted away. "Oh, hey, do you have plans to get a Christmas tree yet?"

"No."

"I'm surprised my mom hasn't invited you to our annual Christmas tree event outing yet. We're going to the tree farm today. A family tradition."

"You mean you don't just buy a fake pre-lit tree like everyone else?"

"Of course not. This is a Wild Harbor tradition. Just wear your warmest flannel, and bring a bow saw."

"I don't even have a bow saw."

"Please don't tell me you've never cut a tree."

He laughed. "I haven't. Is this some kind of Sutton family test I need to pass?"

"According to my dad? Yes. But don't worry. You brought coffee cake, so that will put you on his good side."

"There's one more thing I need to ask." He ran his hand through his hair. He wanted to know where they stood about the date. "It's about the wedding on Saturday." His voice dropped off. He wanted to go with her more than anything. But now he felt like he was wobbling on a tightrope. "I wasn't sure after everything that happened—"

"I would be honored to have you go." A shadow flitted across her face, like clouds over a July sky. "It's just . . ."

"You still want me to go?" He couldn't stop himself. The words tumbled out of him like spilled milk.

Dismay spread across her face. She exhaled hard. "Max, there's something I need to tell you."

Just then, Sophie burst into the room. "Oh, Max, I didn't know you were here." Sophie wrapped her bathrobe around her tighter, then shifted her gaze to Mila as if to ask, *What is he doing here?*

"No, no. It's fine." Mila held up the breakfast treat. "He brought coffee cake." The concern vanished from Sophie's face. Whatever she was about to say could wait.

"Oh, perfect." Sophie snagged the cake from Mila's hands. "You guys all ready for the wedding? I told Grams that Max was coming with you. She was thrilled."

Mila's expression melted into a frown. "You did what?"

"I thought she already knew. But she said you hadn't told her."

"I wanted to surprise her." Mila's tone was like the edge of a knife blade. Sharp and prickly.

"I'm sorry. It slipped." Sophie shrugged.

Mila rubbed her forehead, kneading an unseen pain. "It wasn't how I wanted Grams to find out, but I'll deal with it."

Her sister shrugged, then clicked the door shut.

Max treaded carefully. "So, what was that about?"

"Oh, it's nothing." Her eyes seemed far away, like she was thinking of something.

"You still okay with this?" He couldn't quite figure it out, but something about her seemed off. The glow in her eyes dimmed, snuffed out by some distant, ominous concern.

She nodded, but he didn't believe it. Her reluctance hung in the air between them, sucking oxygen from the room.

There was a reason she didn't want Thelma to know about

him. Had he done something wrong? Did she think Thelma wouldn't approve?

Her face gave nothing away. It was like a shield blocking the light.

He lifted her chin with his hand, trying to find a way in. Her eyelids fluttered in response.

"This is supposed to be fun, remember?" he whispered.

A light sparked in her eyes. "All fun and no romance, right?" Her mouth jerked up in one corner, like she was attempting to smile, but an undercurrent of sadness tinged the edges.

"If that's what you want." He prayed it wasn't.

She didn't respond, leaving the unanswered question hanging between them.

MAX WAS SITTING at the dining room table with a hot cup of coffee when Mila came downstairs, dressed in a sweater and jeans, her hair neatly brushed. She didn't have any makeup on, but her face was freshly scrubbed and her cheeks glowed.

"Finally, we can eat," Sophie teased. "The princess is here."

Mila slugged her sister in his arm as she sat down next to Max. "I got ready faster than you usually do."

"It takes time to look good." Sophie ran her fingers through her hair. "Plus, I'm not used to sharing a bathroom with anyone. I live alone, remember?"

Max had just learned that Sophie was home for Christmas before she'd head back to her job in upstate New York. The Suttons were delighted to have both their daughters in their nest, even if it was temporary.

"Max, we hope you will join us today at the tree farm." Diane served the coffee cake, handing Max a piece first.

"We won't be too hard on you today," Brian added. "As long as you can cut a tree, you'll fit in with the Sutton family."

"Told you," Mila whispered as Diane passed Brian a piece of cake.

"This is divine." Sophie dug into her cake. "Please marry him, Mila. I want this every time I'm home."

Mila's cheeks flushed warm. "You can buy it at the café."

Max took a bite. "We'll sell out by noon. Charlotte can't keep up with the orders this year."

Diane passed around the eggs, bacon, and potatoes, filling plates like it was her duty to stuff them full, like farmhands. Max wasn't used to a big breakfast, if he ate breakfast at all. Sometimes he just drank a cup of coffee while he worked. He remembered the occasional big breakfast with his family when he was young, but when his mom had moved out, Dad had let the boys eat whatever they wanted. After that, every Saturday morning was the same. The boys watched cartoons while gorging on sugary cereal loaded with colorful marshmallows.

He hadn't realized how much he missed a big family breakfast until Brian passed the coffee cake around for seconds. He listened to the chatter of conversation as Diane scooped another round of potato casserole.

He wondered how much he had missed growing up with a single dad who largely let the boys run wild. No family Christmas traditions. No tree cutting. No lights outside or stockings strung across the fireplace. All that had died the day his family crumbled when he was thirteen. Dad's angry outbursts and excessive drinking left massive holes in Max's past, things he couldn't reveal to anyone. No wonder Max couldn't wait to leave home after dealing with it for years. Escaping his past was easier than coping with it.

After college, Max had tried several entrepreneurial adventures and learned how to run a business. He'd finally found success with investment properties, but he couldn't make up for his lack of family. His brother had moved closer to their dad to take care of him, but he never bothered keeping in touch unless he wanted something. His mom, who was noticeably absent from his life after she left, called occasionally, but Max avoided her broken-record messages that pleaded, *Max, this is your mom. Can you call, please?*

No. How could he forgive her for leaving? It had left them all broken in a way that nobody could fix. Not even Max.

"Will you join us today?" Diane startled Max back to the present. "It doesn't matter if you've never cut a tree. Brian will show you. It's time you experienced a Wild Harbor family Christmas tradition."

"This one is fully endorsed by Mila, too." Sophie sat back in her chair.

"What does that mean?" Mila set down her fork.

"You haven't exactly hidden your feelings about the town's winter festival and how it's ruining Wild Harbor." She turned to Max. "I'm in favor of the festival. So whatever Mila says about your plans, don't listen to her."

"Oh thanks, sis," Mila countered. "For your information, we've talked about the festival, and Max has turned me into a reluctant convert."

"A convert, eh? He proved to you he's not making a pile of money off the festival?" Sophie had a bluntness that Mila tried to temper with a look.

"It's not that I'm against the winter festival," Mila argued. "I don't want Wild Harbor to lose its character, like those big beach towns that get overrun by cheap souvenir shops. Wild Harbor needs to embrace what makes it special."

"I think Max is inspiring us all to love Christmas a little more." Diane passed around the eggs and bacon for one more round. "And it wouldn't be Christmas without a stop at the tree farm."

"An artificial tree is not even an option," Sophie reasoned. "The Sutton family has a motto: Go big or go home. I don't understand those people who don't set up a tree."

Mila cleared her throat and gave Max a side-eye. "Leave while you can, Max, before they find out."

"Find out what?" Sophie wasn't about to let Max off the hook.

Max put his napkin on his plate. He might as well confess. "I don't have a tree."

"Like not even a tiny one?" Sophie's eyes looked like they might pop out of her head. Apparently, he had broken some unspoken law of holiday cheer.

"Not even one decoration." Mila was grinning as she plucked her last bite of bacon.

Sophie gasped and covered her face. "You've ruined my entire perception of you as our Christmas hero."

He gave Mila a look. "Thanks for the support. Guilty as charged."

"We need to fix that." Sophie shook her head. "Before anyone finds out. It's not too late." Sophie sipped her juice. "By the way, did you hear the news? Megan got engaged last night."

Diane smiled. "Oh, I'm so happy to hear that. A wedding and an engagement in the same week."

There was a tense pause as Mila headed to the kitchen. Max got up to follow her.

"Everything okay?" She seemed unusually quiet.

"Yeah, I'm fine. I just hate when Mom brings up anything about a wedding. I'm happy for Megan. But I know Mom always thinks of my wedding and what might have been." She shook her head. "At least you've charmed my family. The festival is a big hit with them."

"Unless I can charm you, it doesn't matter." He moved to where she was rinsing dishes in the sink.

The light from the window caught the high ridges of her cheekbones. "Like you said, I don't live here anymore, so why should I care?"

"It's still your home." He leaned his back against the counter so he could see Mila's face. He sensed she was distancing herself. "Your family has traditions, and you don't want someone coming in and ruining them."

"You're not ruining things. Everything is changing. People are getting married. The town is growing. Is it wrong that I wish things would stay like they were when I was a girl?"

"No, but you know what might help that?"

"What?"

Staying. He shook the thought away, afraid to say the words. He didn't want to put pressure on her. Not yet. "Understanding that it's unfair to expect the town won't ever change. Things change. People get married. It's part of life."

"I realize that." She wiped her hands on a towel. "But I don't have to like it."

"Here's my promise to you—I will try to fight for those things that make Wild Harbor special." He took her hands. "For you."

"You'd do that?"

"Of course. After all, I'm willing to hang out with your family at a tree farm, right?"

"Sorry to out you like that, but I knew my sister would freak. Plus, I wanted to see you squirm." She gave him a devious smile. "Are you ready to cut down some trees?"

"Wait, did you say trees? As in plural?"

She nodded. "We're cutting one for you. As the founder of the winter festival, you're not getting out of decorating for Christmas."

"WHAT DO you think of this one?" Brian stopped next to a seven-foot fir that curved awkwardly at the bottom.

Sophie squatted down to examine the trunk. "It looks crooked to me."

"Come over here. This one looks pretty good." Diane was hidden behind a cluster of trees, a few rows away.

Mila linked her arm through Max's and pulled him toward the voice. They had looked at six different trees and still had yet to find the perfect one.

As they zigzagged through a maze of trees, Mila leaned into his body for warmth. "I'm freezing my tail off out here. Are you having fun?"

"I am, but I didn't know how hard it was to find the perfect tree."

She grabbed his gloved hand and pulled him toward a squat, full-bodied fir for a quick inspection. "It doesn't help that my family has different ideas about what perfection is. If we weren't so picky, we'd find one a lot sooner."

In this private spot, he wanted to kiss her, but there was no way he was going to take a chance with her dad around. Plus, he wasn't sure she'd even let him. After their disagreement last night, everything was up in the air. The only reason she seemed to touch him now was because she was cold.

Footsteps trudged down a row next to them as Brian came around the tree and almost walked into them. "Where's Mom?"

Mila shrugged.

"Over here," Mom's muffled voice called out.

They found her standing next to a gigantic tree with a straight trunk and full body. Almost too perfect to be true.

"That one is a beauty." Brian knelt down. "But it's a little big, don't you think? Maybe we should check out some more first."

"Remember the year we left one magnificent tree to find forty duds?" Sophie countered. "We lost the first tree because we couldn't come to a consensus. We ended up buying that horrible tree with the gaping hole in the side."

"Max, what do you say—is this too big?" Brian inspected the trunk.

"Looks good to me. But I've never actually bought one."

"You've never had a tree?" Diane asked incredulously.

"We had one before my mom and dad divorced. But after that, Dad didn't bother decorating for Christmas."

Diane squeezed his elbow. "I'm glad we get the honor of picking out your first tree with you."

"Oh no, this is your tree, not mine." Max stepped away.

"Of course not, honey. You get this one. There are plenty of others."

Brian handed him a saw. "We'll keep looking for ours." The rest of the family started roaming down the adjacent rows, looking for their next tree, leaving Max and Mila alone.

"It'll be beautiful in your apartment." Mila brushed her hands across the prickly needles. Max knelt and chiseled away at the base. "It's not like it's an enormous trunk, but there is something satisfying about this."

His years at home were absent from many father-son activities. He'd never learned to use a saw properly—or any other tools. He had to watch videos on the internet to figure things out. Another way his father had failed him.

The saw sliced an even cut through the trunk as Mila held it steady. After some effort, the tree toppled to the ground.

"Success." Max straightened. "Although I don't know what I'll put on it. I don't own decorations."

"My mom has plenty she doesn't use in the attic. I'm just glad we can get out of the cold now. I'm freezing, and you're like a furnace." She wrapped her arms around him, trying to absorb some of his warmth. Her sudden embrace surprised him, but he instantly leaned into it, burying his nose in her hair. If she was trying to mess with him, she was doing a good job of it.

"You know you can come to my place and just flip a switch on my gas fireplace and the heat is instant."

She frowned. "That's cheating."

"No, it's not. Once you try it, you'll never go back."

"How about as soon as my family finds their tree, we head to your place. We can play Christmas music, light a fire, and you can tell me about your childhood Christmas memories. I know nothing about your family."

Max pulled away from Mila's arms. "There's nothing to tell, really. My childhood wasn't like yours." He didn't want to talk about his past. It was easier to pretend it didn't exist.

Mila wrapped her arms around her body and shivered. "Where do they live now? Do you have any siblings?"

"One older brother and a younger sister who passed away when I was a kid." Max's fingers clenched around the saw.

"Max, I didn't know that. I'm so sorry."

"It was a long time ago." He grabbed the trunk of the fallen tree and lugged it away from her. "I don't keep in touch with my family now," he mumbled over his shoulder.

"But why not?" She jogged to catch up with him. "They're your family."

He ignored her and focused on pulling the tree to the truck.

"Max, why won't you answer me?"

He could hear the bitter voice of his father in his head, *Everyone leaves you eventually, son.* He could see his mom's face of stone the day she left, bitter tears streaming down her cheeks as she told Dad, "You've ruined everything." Then she slammed the door and left.

Max had grown up believing that love meant hurt. Love meant being left alone. Love hadn't been enough to keep his mom from abandoning them. How was that for an explanation?

He plowed forward. "My dad lives in Flint, near where we grew up. My mom lives in Colorado now. I don't talk to her or my brother much."

"Why don't you talk to them?"

"It's complicated." Max plowed ahead, trying to escape her questions. "They've made their decision, and I've made mine. That part of my life is over."

He wasn't ready to explain his brother's betrayal and how

that had severed their relationship. After Mom had left, Caleb had been the only family he'd had left, until that, too, had slipped away. The lesson was not lost on him. The people he loved would always disappoint him.

Everyone leaves you eventually, son.

Mila scrambled to catch up and pulled him to a stop. "I'm sorry, Max. You don't have to talk about it, but I want to understand you more. Couldn't things change?" She searched his face.

"No, they won't." Max's voice was hard as stone. "I don't want to think about it anymore." He turned away as she reached for his arm.

"Max—"

"Would you stop teasing me? Touching my arm, leaning into me. You seriously don't know what you're doing to me, do you?" He turned and blew out of there, stepping between trees, stretching the distance between them like a desert road.

Hope was a false dream. Hope was a deadly arrow. His father's words had stolen everything from him.

CHAPTER ELEVEN

Mila pulled on a lovely red satin dress for the wedding and slid her arms behind her back. Her fingers plucked the zipper and tugged. It stuck at first, and she pulled again. Finally, the zipper caught and slid in an effortless, fluid line up her back. The same way Max's hands gently slipped across her spine like a current.

She twisted her body in the mirror, catching her dazzling reflection. She grasped a diamond earring and secured the back, but her mind was still replaying what had happened yesterday. One minute she had wrapped her arms around Max, and the next, he'd walked away, a dark cloud hovering over his mood.

Her mom peeked around the door.

"You ready to go? Max just pulled up." A tiny, nervous sigh escaped her mother's lips. She wanted things between Mila and Max to work out. She didn't have to say it. Hope was written all over her face.

A car door slammed outside. Her mom rushed to get the door.

The wedding date. She should call Grams and tell her the deal was off.

A doorbell chimed downstairs.

Her fingers hovered over her phone screen and then flicked the call away. She tossed the phone on the bed.

She'd see Grams tonight and pull her aside privately. Why ruin things now?

When she'd made the deal, she'd never considered what would happen if she fell for her date. Her analytical nature had failed to conceive of a hypothetical situation like love. She couldn't imagine this change of heart when she was sprawled on the floor of her office, a pile of overdue bills in her lap.

Now, the guilt was killing her. His warning yesterday had split her in two. *You seriously don't know what you're doing to me, do you?*

He'd looked shaken. It was hard to argue with reality. It was safer if she stayed away after tonight and ignored this chemistry between them. He'd forget about her as soon as she left town.

Animated voices rose up the steps like drifting smoke. Mila slipped on her heels and took one last look in the mirror. She sprayed perfume on the curve of her neck and gave herself a pep talk.

Her ankles wobbled as she descended the steps. She was making a show-stopping entrance, dazzling in her red dress, except this wasn't her moment. This wasn't her wedding. Everything would fall apart after tonight.

Max glanced up the steps and then took a second look. If it had been any other time, Mila would have absorbed that energy and radiated it back like sunlight. But tonight, she could barely muster the courage to stand in front of him. *Little liar.*

No one could make her feel worse than her own conscience. She prayed he'd forgive her for hiding the truth. But if the tables were turned, would she be able to extend the same grace to him?

"Are you ready?" He held out her coat as she slipped her arms into the sleeves. His fingers grazed her bare shoulders.

She swallowed hard. "Yes." Her voice was low and quiet as her eyes cut to her parents. "See you at the wedding."

Mom beamed at Max. Mila could only imagine that she was secretly imagining a budding romance. A lavish wedding. A van full of grandchildren. Her parents' hopes and dreams snowballed in front of her. They wanted so badly to thread the pieces of Mila's life back together after her breakup with Jake.

Max climbed into the car and fingered his key chain, lost in thought. "About yesterday . . ." He couldn't seem to get the words out.

"Max, I'm sorry about what happened."

"No, it's my fault. I'm sorry for how I reacted."

"I won't pressure you to talk about your family, and I'll stay away from now on." She held her hands up. "It's safer that way."

"Safer?" He narrowed his eyes.

"For both of us." Her pulse was elevated just sitting next to him. When it came to Max Malone, safe was what she needed.

"I'm not sure I like playing it safe." He put one hand under her chin and stroked his finger across her jaw. "Especially when you're this stunning. Too bad I have to get you there early to check the bride's dress. Otherwise, I'd steal you away."

"To where?" For someone who'd just committed to staying away, she was entertaining dangerous thoughts.

"I don't know, but I hate to share you with everyone tonight." He winked as the engine roared to life.

When they arrived, Max waited in the foyer as she knocked on the door of the ladies' dressing area.

"I shouldn't be long."

"Take your time." He stretched out on a bench, his long body revealing lean muscle under his suit.

Megan's face peeked out the door. "Wait until you see her. Lily looks amazing."

Lily stood in the mirror, her face dewy and glowing, her dress reflecting the light like a prism in a sunlit window.

As Lily smoothed her hands over the floor-length lace and chiffon gown, Cassidy shook open the long train like a parachute, spreading it behind her sister as it settled to the ground.

Her mother gasped and dabbed her eyes, a tissue clasped between her fingers. She was already crying, and the ceremony hadn't even started. "This dress fits like it was made for you."

"I have Mila to thank for that." Lily nodded toward her friend.

The strapless gown had a fitted, vintage-inspired embroidery and beadwork bodice and a silk chiffon skirt. Becky's floor-length veil capped the gown, the perfect pairing of old and new.

"Everything about you is extraordinary." Megan wrapped her arm around the bride's waist as the girls admired each other in the mirror.

"Don't even get me started." Lily nestled her head against Meg's shoulder. "Once the tears start, they won't stop."

"Here, do you want a tissue?" Her mom pulled one from her purse.

"Where am I going to put that?" Lily held her hand out. "In my bra?"

"You wouldn't be the first." Her mom laughed as Lily dabbed her eyes so she wouldn't mess up her makeup. "My beautiful daughters." She held out her arms and gathered all three girls close. "This is the beginning of so many things. Lily getting married. Megan making wedding plans." She turned to her youngest daughter. "Next, it will be you, Cassidy."

"Mom, it's going to be awhile. I don't even have a boyfriend." Cassidy shook her long blonde locks.

Megan flashed the diamond on her finger. "That means nothing. Finn was the last guy I thought I'd ever date. Surprises happen."

A knock quietly sounded at the door as Matt stuck his head inside. "Everyone dressed and ready? The church is almost full, and Dad is eager to see the bride."

This was a sacred moment. The chance for father and daughter to have a private moment. Mila slipped out, unnoticed by the family. Her job here was done.

Max rose as she approached. "You're frowning," he teased, then stroked a finger across her brow to smooth the wrinkles.

"You don't have to stand for me." She tried to push his strong shoulders down, but he wouldn't budge.

"Of course I will. My mama taught me manners." He almost seemed offended that she'd ask him not to. He offered his arm to her, a silent request to escort her into the sanctuary. She linked her hand through his.

He was so perfect, she was almost fuming. Why did she have to mess up everything with such a nice guy? She could almost taste the acid in her mouth.

"Mila, is that you?" A voice chirped from behind her. *Grams.*

She dropped Max's arm and spun on the heel of her stiletto. This wasn't the way she'd wanted to face her grandmother. Not right before the ceremony.

Grams's eyes swept over Max in his suit. "You did good picking this guy." She winked at Max. A knowing look flashed across her face as she wiggled her eyebrows at Mila.

Max shook his head and laughed. The joy in it was like a shower of confetti.

"She didn't exactly pick me." Max put his hands in his pocket. "I'd say the agreement was mutual." His eyes slid to hers, a private joke between them.

Mila wanted to pull Max into the sanctuary. If he gave away their fake dating arrangement and Grams caught wind of it, she'd out her immediately. Her grandmother never held back her tongue. It was like letting loose a hurricane.

"That was convenient for you, Mila." Grams gave her granddaughter a pat on the arm.

Her body stiffened in response. Two secrets trapped her—keeping her date from finding out about Grams's offer of money and hiding Max's fake date arrangement. Her house of cards was about to fall.

Grams waggled her finger at Max. "Just don't get too frisky on the dance floor."

Mila coughed in embarrassment as Max howled with laughter. Grams was only teasing, but it twisted Mila's insides. She needed to get her grandmother seated before she accidentally let Max know about the money riding on this date.

Max put his hand in between Mila's shoulder blades, sending a shooting spark down her spine. His touch was like a laser bolt of energy. "Thelma, I'm not even sure I want to know what that means. But I can assure you that I'm a gentleman."

"Of course you are. I just wish Mila would have arranged a date as handsome for me." Thelma opened her small, fake-alligator purse with a metal clasp and dug around inside. Mila prayed she wouldn't pull out a check in front of Max.

Her wrinkled lips formed a perfect vowel, then her expression shifted, and she waved her hand in the air. "Never mind. I'll take care of it later. Don't want to miss the ceremony."

She tottered past them into the sanctuary, her eyes scanning the crowd as she looked for a seat.

Mila released her breath like a balloon with a tiny hole. *Too close.* If her grandmother was going to do something rash like offer her money tonight, she needed time to explain things to Max.

When she had agreed to Grams's deal, she'd been imagining some faceless man. The type who wouldn't mind a free meal in exchange for a date. A man who wouldn't light up a single nerve in her body. A boring but tolerable guy. Someone completely forgettable.

Then Max had entered with his disarming steel gaze and a smile that made her legs weak. She'd never thought she would actually get this tangled up in her feelings for him. He was a live wire, shooting sparks every time their eyes met. Danger wrapped in a baby-soft T-shirt. A firebrand sizzling on the surface of her skin. In the coming months, she'd replay these dates over in her mind like some kind of stalker. Except she wasn't a stalker at all. She just kept rewinding every fatal flaw she'd made in this disastrous relationship. Her biggest one? Agreeing to Grams's deal.

Her second one? Falling for a man before she was ready to trust again. The whole thing was a train wreck.

She couldn't let Max think she had used him as her date to keep her shop afloat. But confessing the truth made her want to sprint to the car. She'd speed back to Chicago and never look back.

Resolve glued her feet to the floor. She'd look like a crazy person if she ran out now.

She needed to get through this wedding first. Sit as far away from Grams as possible and avoid any contact for the rest of the night.

"Should we sit down?" Mila grabbed Max's arm, dragging him away from the aisle where Grams sat. She scanned the sanctuary like a map and chose the opposite corner.

She sank down in the pew without asking if he'd like a different view. He followed without comment because that's the type of date Max was. Along for the ride.

The string quartet soared as the ceremony unfolded like a Christmas dream, every bridesmaid draped in brilliant deep red, contrasting with the bride's winter-white dress that shimmered in the candlelight. The way Lily and Alex looked at each other nearly undid Mila. Her heart felt wrung out until it was an empty shell. She willed the tears to stop, but they kept leaking from her eyes. She smeared her makeup with a tissue.

What was wrong with her? Love seemed like such a dazzling thing, an illuminated vision that was blinding and consuming her at the same time.

After the ceremony, the crowd drifted over to a gorgeous reception hall that looked out over the water. Guests mingled around tables, and Mila found herself surrounded by people drilling her with questions about her shop in Chicago or cornering Max, asking about his development plans. They pinwheeled through the crowd, losing each other, but waving from across the room, separated by what felt like miles of people. When the emcee announced dinner, they shuttled off toward round tables with elaborate floral displays. She dreaded being pinned to a table with her grams and prayed she was not.

A hand found her back, and she turned, startled by the feel of someone's palm on her bare skin. *Max.* A zing of energy shot through the space between her shoulder blades. His hand was like fire on her flesh.

"Fancy meeting you here," he joked with a straight face.

They'd been separated for only a half hour, but it felt like days. How did he wreck her with a touch?

"Do you have a date tonight?" she teased back, leaning against the wall next to a potted plant. In this corner of the ball-room, she'd found a quiet, little paradise.

He played along. "She left me behind, even though I struck a deal with her. Haven't seen her since. I want my money back."

"Pity. Maybe I can fill in?"

"You'll do, all right." He winked.

His flirting was dangerous, leaving her heart twisting inside out. Why did he have to be so charming?

She cleared her throat, ready to confront the guilt that was slowly strangling her. "Max, about that deal we made . . ."

"Yes?" His eyes flicked to hers and she suddenly felt exposed, like a fraud. He wouldn't look at her the same anymore once he knew the truth. That razzle-dazzle magic he did on her heart would sizzle out like a wet towel over a match.

"I don't want you to feel obligated to be with me tonight. The agreement we made—you can call it off."

The doubt clouded his eyes. "Do you not want me to be your date?"

"Oh, no." She took a step toward him and her drink splattered across the arm of his suit coat. "I'm sorry." She dabbed a few spots of iced tea from his jacket with her napkin. "It's just that . . ." She swallowed hard. Her eyes lifted to his steel-blue gaze. The color of the sky after a storm. The blue spark of electricity. She never wanted to forget the shade that unraveled her from within. Her heart unspooled like cotton.

"Mila!" a voice interrupted before she could get the words out. Edna Long held a paper with a diagram of tables. As the unofficial town matron, she had volunteered to help with coordinating the wedding and reception—a job she relished. "You're at our table with your family, and it's time to start."

She took Mila's elbow and steered her toward the table with Grams, Sophie, and her parents. Her dad waved like a desperate motorist stranded on the side of the highway. Normally, this table would have been an easy arrangement of familiar people, but her body stiffened as she saw the only chairs left were next to Grams.

It was too late to change, and she'd have to force the conversation away from any talk of dating. With her grams, that might be next to impossible.

"Don't you two look like the perfect couple?" Edna's red lips suppressed a smile as she swished her lemonade around with a straw, the ice clinking against the glass.

Thelma took a swig of iced tea and grimaced at the glass. "I'd bet money that Mila catches the bouquet." She plucked a packet of sweetener and dumped it in her tea.

Mila's body prickled with heat. "I don't think I want to catch the bouquet." Her voice was as blunt as a dull file. She needed to steer this topic away from marriage. That subject was like stepping onto a minefield.

Her finger circled the top of her glass. "Doesn't Lily look extraordinary?"

"Like a younger version of Becky Woods." Edna clinked her ice some more. She'd seen so many weddings through the years.

Mom snagged a dinner roll and broke it in half, then slathered a dollop of butter on top. "Her dress was perfect, Mila. I know how much she appreciated you coming home for this."

"How is the shop doing?" Edna dug into a plate of chicken surrounded by tiny round potatoes the size of golf balls.

"Oh, it's an adventure." Mila zeroed in on her plate as she sliced chicken. Stab. Slice. Repeat. A mist of sweat broke out across her forehead.

"Chicago is mighty expensive." Edna pierced her potato with her fork and held it dangling mid-air.

Please let this conversation die or I might have to. Mila's mouth felt full of gritty sand.

"It is." She scooped up her water and downed half a glass before she choked on the last swallow. As she sputtered, Grams walloped her back.

"I'm fine," she croaked. She wasn't fine. This whole charade was getting to her.

Maybe if she choked to death, she could veer the conversation away from her shop. A tap on the shoulder jolted her back to the present. It was Cassidy, her long blonde curls cascading down her back, her lips set in a red stain. Cassidy should have been swept away by some gorgeous guy long ago. Even though Wild Harbor wasn't a big town, she'd always turned heads. She could have any guy she wanted.

"Lily asked to have you join us for a picture. Would you mind?" She grinned, and a dimple on her left cheek deepened. Mila had always envied Cassidy's single, adorable dimple.

"Not at all." She scooted her chair back and dropped her red napkin next to her half-eaten plate. She wasn't hungry today, anyway. Guilt had dulled her appetite. "Excuse me. I'll be back in a few minutes."

She fell into step next to Cassidy and only looked back once. Edna was talking, her hands flapping around like wings.

They headed to the corner of the room where Megan, Lily, and Aspen were already posing for the photographer. Cass pulled on her arm as they fell into place next to the other girls. "Max and you are really lovely together."

She didn't bother answering. If she glanced at her friend now, Cass would read her feelings like it was imprinted across her forehead.

"Mila, is something wrong?" Concern tinged Cassidy's whisper.

Mila locked on to the camera and held her pose. "We're not together. Not that way." She tilted her chin toward the photographer. Her smile froze.

"Stop sabotaging yourself. He's nice, and I can tell by how he looks at you that there's something there." She pinched Mila's side.

"Ow," Mila blurted out at the shock of her friend's fingernails.

The photographer snapped a picture.

"Oh, great. That's going to be a wonderful picture of me making a hideous face."

"They'll delete it. Maybe you should come home on weekends." Cassidy pasted on a smile and held her pose again.

"I'm not sure Max will want to see me after the holidays." A blinding light exploded and Mila blinked.

Cass turned to Mila, her smooth brow etched with wrinkles. "You can't say that. You don't know."

Mila's gaze cut to Max. Grams had scooted closer to her date and was telling him an animated story.

Max was absorbed, a sponge soaking up Thelma's every word.

No one else at the table seemed to listen. They were all in their own worlds. Conversations spinning like planets orbiting across solar systems. One tiny catastrophic shift in the universe and everything would be thrown off course.

Max frowned, and his eyes swept over to Mila for a brief second. Dismay spread across his face. Mila didn't need to ask Grams what she had told him. The second she saw his look, she knew.

Mila's world tilted like half of the floor had just collapsed. She stumbled forward, the room spinning.

Max stood quickly and headed toward the exit.

Mila rushed to stop him, zigzagging between tables and servers like an obstacle course, almost causing one poor busboy to drop an entire tray of dirty plates.

Max wasn't supposed to find out this way.

She had to reach him before he left, if only to explain her side of the story before her world spun out of control.

"Max!" Her voice sounded ragged, like threads being pulled out by desperation.

Max paced the sidewalk, refusing to turn her way. She could tell by the slump of his shoulders that something was wrong.

"I want to explain." Her lungs burned in the frozen air.

He swiveled to face her. Anger flashed across his expression. "Thelma already told me."

"About?" She needed to hear how bad it was. All the sordid details. Grams wasn't one to leave anything out.

"She told me she agreed to give you money if you found a date for the wedding. It was a financial arrangement. I thought this was becoming something more. So, congratulations on your performance, Mila. You had me totally fooled."

He bolted forward, but she grabbed his coat sleeve, urging

him to stay. She swung around, orbiting him like the sun. He had always pulled her in this way.

"No, wait. You need to hear me out." She grasped his hand, desperate to keep him here.

"I've already heard everything I need to know." He pulled his hand back.

"When we made this agreement, I didn't even know you. It seemed like a mutual arrangement. You wanted Lexy off your back."

He frowned. "I thought you wanted people to know you were over Jake. It seemed like an even exchange."

Her heart withered at the disdain in his voice. "It's true I wanted people to think that. We both had our reasons. I didn't bring up Grams's offer because I didn't think it would go this far. I thought we were going out for one date."

"Then why didn't you tell me later? After I asked you out for real?"

"I wanted to. My plan was to tell you tonight after I pulled Grams aside to tell her the deal was off. But I lost my nerve. I thought you'd despise me if I told you about the money. You'd believe I was using you."

"You *were* using me, Mila." His voice erupted like an angry hiss.

"I could say the same of you." She matched his body position. Hands on hips. Chin raised. Eyes narrowed.

"That's not what tonight was. At least, not for me."

"Hasn't it been convenient that you've had a date to all these events? I've been an easy fill-in for you. A substitute for an actual relationship. Come on, Max, it's not like you're totally innocent here."

"You were never a substitute." His laser blue eyes were pinning her down, cutting her into pieces. "I asked you out because I wanted something more between us."

"Oh." Her tongue stuck to the roof of her mouth. "I thought you wanted me to keep my distance. Remember?"

He choked out a sarcastic half-laugh and sat on a bench. "I don't think you fully understood what I meant."

"Then explain it. Because you've never told me how you really feel."

"You're wrong. I've told you every chance I could. There is nothing I wouldn't do for you." His head slid down as he covered his face with his hands. "What an idiot I am."

If he'd struck her, she couldn't have hurt more. "Max, you think I did this on purpose to hurt you? That was never my intent. You don't know how I feel about you." She inched down to him and prayed he wouldn't walk away.

He stared hard at her, his blue eyes dark. "Tell me the truth, then. How do you feel about me?"

She grabbed the bench so he wouldn't see her hands shake. She was about to free-fall off a cliff. If she didn't tell him now, she might lose him forever.

"Scared that if I let you into my world, you'd become it." She waited to see if he would reject her for good.

She caught a flicker in his expression. A desperate, dying spark.

He reached his hand to her arm and slid it from elbow to wrist. Then he wrapped her fingers in his. The spark flared with heat. "I don't understand why you didn't just tell me."

"I was afraid you wouldn't believe me. You had me cornered."

He lifted his eyebrows.

"Okay, I had myself cornered. I'm the idiot here, not you." She slumped back on the bench. She'd probably lost Max for good. There was no use hiding anything from him now. "Just so you know, I'm not taking Grams's money."

"Why didn't you tell me you were in financial trouble?"

"And make myself look like even more of an idiot? No, thank

you. I've already endured the humiliation of closing my shop once. If I close in Chicago, at least it's a big enough city that no one would notice. But I can't come home with my tail between my legs. Not again."

His lips tightened. "Why not?"

"I'd start over somewhere else, even if that meant working at a truck stop again."

An image twisted inside her brain from college, truckers catcalling her on the job. She couldn't go back to that dismal prospect. She'd paper the city with job applications instead, and cling to the phone, hoping for a break.

"I'd take you anytime at the French Press." His face spread into a soft grin. He was flirting with her, and she couldn't tear her eyes away from him. "Free coffee and a lot of time with yours truly."

"Tempting. If I get desperate, I'll find you." She licked her lips.

His eyes dropped to them.

"I'll be waiting for your call." The way he looked at her now made her want to accept the invitation. He was playing it safe. Trying to let her down easy.

She bit her lip, not ready to say goodbye. She'd never let him go if she didn't do it now. "Well, it was nice getting to know you, Max." She held her hand out, waiting for him to shake it.

"Nice?" He pushed her hand away. "You deserve more than a handshake." He cupped her face in his hand, leaned forward, and planted a kiss on her cheek. It was warm and soft. Not a goodbye kiss, but an invitation. If she hadn't just ruined their relationship, she'd say yes to whatever he was offering her.

She leaned back, entranced by the warmth radiating on her cheek. "I guess this is it." She wasn't good at leaving. Her legs stuck to the bench.

"Can we start over?"

"What do you mean?"

"Hi, I'm Max." He put his hand out.

What was this game? She swatted his hand away. "Someone told me you deserve more than a handshake." His mouth twitched, but he kept a straight face.

"But I don't even know your name." His face was serious while his eyes danced with pleasure.

"Max. Stop." She gave him a tiny shove.

"That's my name. What's yours?" He was forcing her to role-play. A chance to rewind time and start over.

"I'm Mila. Pleased to meet you."

"Mi-la." He rolled the word in his mouth like he was savoring it. "Beautiful." He took her hand and kissed the back of it. The current of his touch spread along the length of her arm. She felt like she was glowing as brightly as an Edison bulb.

"Does this mean you don't hate me forever?" Her tone was filled with wonder and confusion. She silently pleaded for him to say no.

"How could I hate you? We've only just met." He took her hands in his and dropped a smile that nearly undid her.

So this was what forgiveness felt like.

He wrapped his hand around her bare shoulder as she leaned into the curve of his arm. They fit together perfectly.

"Mila, would you go out with me sometime? No strings attached?" He rested his cheek against her hair as the stars showered them with light.

"Yes." She followed his gaze to the burning orbs above. "No strings attached."

CHAPTER TWELVE

MAX

Max had just finished grinding coffee beans when a familiar voice echoed a morning greeting across the café. A rich, robust scent combined with nutty aromatic middle notes permeated the room. It was a smell that Max never tired of. The first scent of morning.

Joshua was always the first customer on weekdays, grabbing his coffee before he disappeared for the morning. Sometimes he went fishing. Other days to his cabin on the lake.

Joshua's weathered hands fiddled with a small leather wallet falling apart at the seams. He frequently brought in the strangest items from his salvage shop. Pocket watches and old silverware. Cracked glass trinkets and old hinges from doors. Where he got them, Max didn't have a clue. But the man seemed to have this uncanny knack for knowing how to fix things, and he relished showing Max his latest restoration. But even more disconcerting was his ability to read Max, as if he could see under the surface of his skin, like he was transparent. Max didn't have to tell Joshua when something was bothering him, when the ugly threads from his past were snaking through him again. Joshua just knew.

"Coffee smells good." Joshua swept his fingers over the wallet, the pads of his fingers smoothing the scratched leather.

As Joshua reached for a cup, a deep scar across his wrist peeked out beyond his shirt sleeve. It was jagged and puckered, an old injury that had healed over, leaving behind the remnants of a painful wound.

Max looked away. Why was ugliness so painful to witness? He focused on filling Joshua's cup, but his eyes flicked back to the scar. "You never told me what happened to your wrist."

Joshua adjusted his sleeve to cover it. "That's a story for another day." His lips turned up at the corners. "I brought you something I think you'll find interesting." He tossed the wallet on the counter. "It's your father's."

"How do you know my dad?" Max picked up the wallet and turned it over in his fingers. It didn't look worth keeping, but something about it seemed familiar.

"I don't. His name is on it."

"You found my dad's old wallet?" Max slid the cup across the counter.

"In a bin of castaways. Most of it was junk until I found that. Thought you could take it to your dad."

"I don't see my father anymore." Max's tone was sharp, like a voice he once knew. A person he had blocked from his mind.

"Is that so?" Joshua tipped his cup. "Pass it along to someone else in your family. A mother or sibling, perhaps?"

"I don't talk to them much. Like you said, it's a story for another day."

A flicker crossed Joshua's face. "I guess we all have those." Joshua didn't press the subject. "Bring Mila to the shop some-time. I have something to show her." His footsteps echoed as he left the café, escaping into the darkness of morning.

Max ran his hand through his hair, then tucked the wallet in his pocket. When he'd chosen Wild Harbor, it had been because he had no past tied to this place. But Joshua had caught up to him, forcing him to circle back and face his own demons.

Max's phone buzzed as his brother's name appeared on the screen.

Caleb: Dad's health isn't good. He's asking to see you for Christmas.

A hard knot rose in his throat. Max's response was swift and final. *No.*

Couldn't Caleb understand he had a business to run? It's not like he could leave whenever he pleased. Driving two hours wasn't an option.

He sent the one-word text and slid his phone across the counter.

He hadn't spoken to his dad since he'd moved to Wild Harbor. His family's unresolved issues had split them apart.

His phone rang, vibrating against the countertop. Caleb wouldn't leave him alone unless he answered. He knew how this game worked.

"Hey, it's going to be rush hour in here soon."

"Well, good morning to you too." His brother didn't hide his sarcasm. "Is that the way you greet everyone?"

"Only you." Max dumped old coffee grounds in the trash. "I'm working right now, and you never call unless you want something."

"I never call unless it's *important*," Caleb corrected. "If you called Dad every once in a while, I wouldn't have to. It's just being considerate."

Max kicked the toe of his shoe against the trash can. His brother portrayed himself as a saint, but Max knew better.

"If you're so considerate, then why did you date Taylor after me? Because last I checked, that's not something a brother would do."

He heard a long pause, then the rustle of something in the background. Caleb wasn't alone.

"I'm not calling to talk about Taylor," his brother responded without emotion. His way of proving he was bulletproof. "Just to set the record straight, I didn't steal Taylor. She had broken up with you. She made her choice."

Max stared at the wall, wanting to hit something. *Hard.* His brother would never apologize or admit he was wrong. Even though his feelings for Taylor had faded, the resentment between brothers had snowballed. He rolled his hands into fists and squeezed until they hurt.

"You've always been good at making excuses. This conversation is over unless you have more to say."

"Did you see my text about Dad? He wants to see you over the holidays."

"I'm not coming. I thought I made that clear."

"He's on hospice, Max. They haven't even given him a month."

The news slammed into Max like a wall. Now it was his turn to appear bulletproof. He steadied his voice. "A month."

"He may not even live a week."

Max leaned against the wall, the back of his head pressed against the cool surface. He didn't want to explain their complicated relationship. "He wasn't really a dad to me. You didn't see what I did."

His older brother was seventeen when their sister had died. Caleb had left home a year later, and missed the angry, drunken rages and the arguments between their parents. Everything had soured after the funeral, like rotten milk.

"He's still your dad." His brother's voice turned hollow.

"I'll let you know if I change my mind." Max wasn't about to make any promises. Instead, he'd become a master at knee-jerk reactions. If Caleb swung a fist, he had to swing back.

He walked out of the storage room where Lexy waited in the corner.

"You don't look good." Lexy's eyes narrowed as she followed his path across the café.

"Good guess." What was the point of hiding his foul mood? She'd figure it out, anyway.

She sauntered toward him, an animal sniffing out blood. "Anything I can do to help?"

"I'm fine. Just family stuff. You know, complicated."

"How so?" She leaned on the counter, settling in for his response.

The story tumbled out before he could stop it. For all her faults, she was a good listener. "My brother called and told me that my father doesn't have much time. He's still mad I won't visit. But he doesn't know how bad it was after our parents separated. My dad left me to fend for myself at thirteen."

She listened in silence, then circled around the counter and wrapped her arms around him. She pulled away to look at him, her arms still secured around his waist as a group entered the café. He stepped away, but it was too late. A few eyes darted from him to her.

Lexy leaned back against the counter. "I hear you went to the wedding with Mila?"

"Yeah." He turned away from her and measured out more coffee, unable to shake her.

"What happens when she goes back to Chicago?"

"Haven't talked about it yet."

"I saw her walking home the night the skating rink opened. I wondered what was up."

Customers were staring at them. "Good thing that's not your business." He gave her a tight smile. "I need to make more coffee. Will you excuse me?" He started to cross around her, but she blocked his way.

"Whatever you decide, I'm here, okay?" She touched his arm.

An ambulance siren wailed in the distance. Max's muscles tensed. He slipped to a back storage room and sat down on the floor until the siren passed.

He pulled out the wallet that Joshua had given him. The leather was stretched thin, like an old hide. As he opened it, a faded photograph fluttered to the floor. A man held a little girl, her cheeks pink in the sunlight, curls folding around her face in delicate spirals. Folds of baby fat lined her wrists, and her chunky sausage hand grasped a dandelion.

He'd know those eyes anywhere.

Eyes he hadn't seen since the day the sirens had taken her away. She had been playing in the yard when her ball rolled across the driveway. Mom had stepped inside for a second, while Dad backed out the car to go to work. In that moment, his little sister's life had been taken.

His father had become a shell of his former self, wrapped in grief, unable to pick up the pieces of his shattered life. Mom blamed Dad for the accident and their marriage disintegrated, the way a jack-o-lantern slowly rots from the inside. Max hadn't understood the complexities of loss back then. All he knew was that grief could break you.

Fifteen years later, he still avoided the memories. But they kept chasing him down, dogging him for something he did not want to give.

As he held his head in his hands, a text roused him.

Mila: I'd still love to go with you to the gala this weekend, if you want me to be your guest?

Like there was any question. He'd have her a thousand times over if she asked him.

But his dad's voice looped in his mind, *Everyone leaves you eventually, son.*

She was going back to Chicago soon. Why should he risk it all for her?

As much as he wanted to push her away, he ignored the voice in his head, the one that told him not to take a chance. The one that reminded him she would still leave anyway.

CHAPTER THIRTEEN

Maybe it was good she wouldn't see Max this morning. The way things had ended at the wedding had left an expanding uncertainty between them. Time away would give Mila a chance to figure out what she really wanted, even though everything told her it was Max.

Today, though, she couldn't think about him. She was focused on fitting Megan for a wedding dress, which had required her to make a quick trip to Chicago. Work would take her mind off of Max, but after a day of her phone being oddly silent, she felt unsettled and lonely.

Why hadn't he responded? He was like a craving she couldn't ignore.

Mila arrived at the Woods family's home around two with a stack of dresses in her arms. Megan's black hair curled loosely around her shoulders, and her long, dark lashes framed her copper eyes. Even though she and Lily were different, Megan would make an equally gorgeous bride.

"I hope you like the dresses I brought as much as the pictures online." Mila draped the gowns across the sofa.

"Thank you so much for fitting in Megan today and going to all this trouble." Becky wrapped an arm around Mila's waist. "Finn took Bill to his doctor's appointment so I could be here for Megan."

"I'm so glad. Dress fittings are my favorite part." She carefully unzipped one of the dress bags. The gown shimmered in the light.

"It's too beautiful to try on." Megan shook her head as she touched the delicate lace.

"This is part of the fun." Mila handed the dress to Megan. "It will be even more beautiful when you're wearing it. Do you want my help?"

"No." Megan grabbed Cassidy's arm. "Cass is going to help me. Put your feet up and relax." The sisters disappeared into the bedroom.

"I made a fresh pot of coffee. Can I pour you a cup?" Becky motioned to Mila.

"Sure, I'd love that." Mila sat down at the island as Becky poured coffee.

"So how are you?" Becky leaned across the island, setting the cup in front of her. "It seems like things are going well for you since you met Max."

Mila nearly choked on her coffee. "Uh, well. He's nice." Her face grew warm. She wasn't about to explain how she had almost ruined everything.

Becky poured herself a cup and sat next to Mila. "I have to admit, all the girls in my book club are jealous. They think you'll steal him away to Chicago."

"We're not really that serious, and to be honest, I'm not sure I'm ready for anything long term." Some days it felt like Jake had ruined her for good. She wanted to trust Max, but a part of her still resisted.

"Well, when you head back to the city, I wouldn't recommend staying away for long. There are some girls who aren't afraid of stealing a boyfriend."

Mila didn't need a warning. Her breakup with Jake had already taught her how fragile relationships were. "I know you're watching out for me, but Max has a good head on his shoulders."

Becky paused as if she was wrestling with a thought. "I'm sure it's nothing to be concerned about, but yesterday morning I saw him talking with Lexy, and something struck me as odd."

Mila's mouth went dry. "Why would that be odd?" She tried to hide her worry.

"When we walked into the café, her arms were around him."

This couldn't be happening again. The image of Max and Lexy burned into her mind. She wanted to trust Max and not jump to conclusions, but it was hard with her past. "I'm sure there was a reason."

Becky's eyes softened. "I know it's been hard to trust someone new after Jake. But if you're serious about Max, I'm afraid that staying away isn't a good option."

A small ripple of panic flowed through Mila. She'd deal with this unsettling news later.

Cassidy opened the door. "Are you both ready?"

"Whenever you are." Becky climbed off her stool.

Megan stepped out from the bedroom, transformed by the dress. Every curve was draped in white lace, shimmering like silver snow as she walked toward them.

Becky gasped. "Oh, Megan, it's beautiful."

"What do you think?" Megan's eyes brightened.

There was something calming about seeing a bride for the first time. A reminder that love could win out after all.

"I think it's perfect." Mila's eyes filled with tears.

Megan deserved every bit of happiness. For now, she would witness an intimate moment between mother and daughter.

Becky wiped a tear from her cheek as she took her daughter's hands in hers. A mother remembering her tiny baby and seeing the woman she had become. A full-circle moment.

Mila sat in silence, honored to be a part of this special milestone, even if she would never have her own.

MILA PUT another ornament on the tree, her mind far away, thinking of her date for the gala on Friday. The lingering doubts she had about him still hung over her like a dark cloud. It had been her sister's idea to sneak over to Max's apartment and decorate his tree while he worked. He wouldn't be home until evening and had conveniently shown her where he hid the spare key the night of the ice-skating accident.

His apartment reminded her of the night he had kissed her. His warm lips on hers. The crashing wave that warned her to stay away. If she returned now, her heart wouldn't be too badly damaged. She had fallen hard for him, but she still couldn't shake the fear that he would trample on her, just like Jake had.

When she'd looked at Megan's shining face in her wedding gown, she'd had to beat down that deep longing to be loved. Ignore it. Smother it. She would never possess that happiness for herself. Not with all the baggage she carried, thanks to Jake.

Sophie hung a shiny silver ornament on the bottom of the tree, then glanced sideways at Mila, her eyes mapping out her mood. "How are you feeling about Max?"

Mila shrugged.

Her sister would see through any excuses she made. They had the kind of relationship where they couldn't hide secrets.

Sophie plucked another bulb. "I'm happy you're dating again. Max is a great guy."

"I think so." Mila hung another ornament on a branch, unsure how to say it.

Sophie cocked her head. "Think? You don't sound like someone who is falling in love. Is there something you're not telling me?"

She knew her sister wouldn't let her off easy. "There's nothing to tell. It's just hard."

"What do you mean? Love isn't hard at the beginning. It should be easy at this point. Love gets hard when you're in it for the long haul."

"So, you're the relationship expert now?"

"No, I'm just saying that you either like him or you don't."

She had her reasons for not rushing into things. "I'm just not sure if I can trust him."

"Why? Has he given you a reason not to trust?"

Mila let out a heavy sigh as she put a gold Christmas bulb on the tree. "Becky told me she saw Max and Lexy hugging at the coffee shop. It's not fair, Sophie. Every time I fall for a guy, Lexy sets her sights on him. I don't understand it. First Jake, now Max. Why couldn't she get married, so I wouldn't have to worry about it anymore?"

"Oh, I don't think a wedding ring would stop Lexy. That's exactly why Jake didn't marry her."

Mila shook her head. "I don't think so."

"If Max has any brain in his head, he'll see what an idiot she is. But that doesn't excuse you from letting him know how you really feel."

"I can't do that. I'm heading back to Chicago after the holidays. It will never work."

"Maybe you should worry less about how it's going to work and more about whether he's the right man. Because if he is, you'll find a way to make it work. You're still going to the gala with him tomorrow, right?"

"I told him I would, but—" She flopped down on the couch. The same couch where he'd kissed her.

"Mila, you're not backing out. Don't let fear make your decision. Promise me you'll give him a chance."

Why was love so hard? All she wanted was to protect herself from more pain. Being alone meant she was safe.

She tucked a stray wisp of hair over her ear. "I don't know. I want to—I really do." Sadness draped over her like an old coat.

Her sister wrapped her arms around her, leaning her forehead into Mila's hair. It was something they'd done as girls when one of them was sad.

"I know you do," Sophie whispered. "I don't want you to throw away a great guy because someone has hurt you before. At least give him one more try. Go to the gala. One last date."

"I can survive one more date. But unless you're my fairy godmother, I don't have a thing to wear. I wasn't planning on attending a gala when I packed for this trip."

"Are you giving me a challenge? As your official fairy godmother, I know the perfect place we can go shopping tomorrow. There's an adorable new boutique downtown called Bella's. As long as I can find you a dress, you're going to the gala."

A GIRL MUST HAVE the right pair of shoes to go with her dress. This is the first rule of getting dressed up.

So when Sophie held up a fancy pair of rhinestone heels at Bella's, Mila sensed they weren't right. Not for a winter event or the dress she had picked. She shook her head in protest.

When Sophie tried again, this time with some stellar dress boots, Mila was sold. She had always been a boot girl.

Her dress was rose gold, cut at the knees so it would show off the boots.

"You know, I never would have picked that dress for myself,

but the color and style are perfect for you. You're gorgeous," Sophie gushed.

Celeste, the shop owner, had agreed. Immaculately dressed in an all-black ensemble, Celeste had studied fashion in Paris and then opened her shop in Wild Harbor.

"Dozens of girls have tried on that dress, but it hasn't been right for any of them," Celeste confessed. "Until you came in."

Mila admired her dress in the mirror one last time before she left. It was beautiful, but she didn't want Max to fall for her because of a dress. She wanted him to choose her because she was the one.

"Is it too much?" Mila spun around. "I'm not the type of girl who wants to be in the spotlight. I'm a wallflower who wants to hide in the corner."

Sophie leaned forward and put her hands on Mila's arms. "Not tonight."

Mila pulled up to the gala in her new boots and dress, her heart thumping like a bass drum. Could she really just fix the banged-up pieces of her heart? Her life was a mess. Her wedding dress still hung in her closet. Nobody wanted to take on the disaster that was Mila Sutton.

She whispered a prayer for help and forced herself to walk into the ballroom. It was now or never.

The foyer twinkled with blue lights across the ceiling, giving the effect of a starry night, while stunning Christmas trees flanked the doors. People gathered in groups, laughing. She took a deep breath. One foot in front of the other.

A live band started a rendition of "Blue Christmas" with an alto saxophone wailing sultry notes across the dance floor. The white and blue Christmas lights reflected off the rose gold sparkle on Mila's dress, making her shimmer in the light. She scanned the room for Max, but it was hard to pin anyone down in the crush of the crowd.

Then she sensed the heavy stare of someone's eyes locked on

her. She glanced around to find Max's intense gaze burning into her. He moved across the ballroom, meeting her halfway, closing the space between them so that she wouldn't have to make the rest of the trek alone. He took her hands. His touch was electrifying.

"I've always thought you were beautiful, but tonight you look incredible. I'm the luckiest guy here."

"I'm not used to getting dressed up like this. Can I go back home and put my jeans on?" She tucked a stray tendril over her ear. Her sister had wrangled her hair in a fancy updo with gently curled wisps framing her face.

"That's surprising, coming from you—the woman who sells fancy dresses for a living. Don't you ever try them on just for fun?"

"Absolutely not. It's a promise I made to myself after the Jake fiasco." Mila turned away, remembering her first dress, the one that still hung in her closet like a broken promise. She should let it go, but an inner force resisted giving it up. Until she found the right guy, the one who would thread together the pieces of her heart, it would continue to remind her of what she had lost.

"I'm sorry. I didn't mean to bring it up." Max brushed his fingers across her back. "Would you like to dance with me?"

Mila couldn't keep from smiling. He had a way of lighting her up. "I'd love that."

He took her hand and led her to the dance floor. The band had begun a Christmas ballad as couples streamed onto the dance floor, swaying in rhythm to the saxophone.

Mila hadn't danced since high school prom and wasn't sure she could remember what to do with her body. She was a tangled mess of awkward legs and feet, but when Max wrapped his arms around her waist, she fell into a natural rhythm with him. Enveloped in his arms, all her thoughts about the wedding dress in her closet faded. For the first time, she didn't push away her feelings for Max. This was what she longed for—the sense that nothing could hurt her when she was with him. Instead of fleeing from his closeness, she let herself lean into him, enjoying the scent of his skin and the warmth of his embrace.

"I'm sorry for how we ended the day at the tree farm," Max whispered, his cheek against her hair. "I want to tell you more about my family, but it's still hard to talk about."

Mila leaned back, and a flicker of sadness crossed his face. He hadn't pushed her away because he was rejecting her. He had shielded his feelings because he didn't want her to see his hurt.

She stopped moving. "I had no idea what I was asking. When you're ready to talk, I'll be here."

"I want to, but first I need to do something." His voice dropped, but there was a promise in his eyes. A hope for reconciliation. Mila realized that now.

Max leaned close. "It's hard for me to concentrate when you're this close," he whispered into her ear. He brushed his hand across her jawline, causing shivers to erupt over her skin. "By the way, why haven't we walked the beach together yet?"

"It's been snowing. Not exactly beach weather."

"I love the beach during different seasons, especially when the ice settles on the lake. Promise me we'll go out on the balcony tonight and look at the lake?"

The thought of leaving was something she'd pushed to the back of her mind. After the holidays, she would pack up and say goodbye, and then what? Their relationship was still in limbo while the clock counted down the seconds until this fairy tale would end. But unlike Cinderella's stroke-of-midnight deadline, there was no magic that would make everything better.

"I promise," she whispered as the music hit a melancholy note. She rested her head on his shoulder, not wanting to think about her dwindling time with Max. Hadn't she promised herself one last date before she said goodbye?

His hand enveloped hers as he pulled her toward the

balcony. "Let's see it now. It might not be like taking a stroll on the beach, but the lake is beautiful."

A clear, moonlit evening greeted them as they left the crowd and snuck outside. The snow from the previous day had settled on the ground in a blanket of white, and the shining, smooth surface glowed like a clean sheet. Everything looked prettier when it was cloaked in white. The brown foliage was hidden away. The ugliness of winter covered up. If only she could do the same with her life.

In the distance, the lake shimmered like a mirror. She stared, transfixed, at the white landscape until she realized Max was no longer admiring the view. Instead, he had shifted his gaze to her, and his hand brushed her cheek, sliding down to her chin, cupping it slightly. With his other hand, he touched her bare shoulder and then dropped it down to her waist, where he wrapped his arm around her. He leaned forward, and his lips suddenly found hers.

It had been so long since she'd let herself enjoy a moment like this. The warmth of his kiss left her longing for him to do it again.

"I've been wanting to do that ever since I kissed you the first time. But I didn't know if you wanted it too."

She nodded, falling completely under his spell.

"Can I kiss you again?" he asked gently.

She nodded again. His hand slid to the curve of her neck as he leaned forward and his lips found hers again. The warmth of his hand on her back caused her mind to spin in circles. It was like she was on a rope swing that had been wound tight, slowly twirling until the tension released.

He reluctantly pulled back, a smile playing on his lips. "Wow. I can't believe I'm about to say this, but I'm so glad you hit me on my bike."

She shook her head. "Really? I still feel terrible about it."

"Don't. I'd do it again if I had to. That's how much I want to be with you" He ran his fingers up her arm. "You're shivering. Let's go back inside to warm up."

They walked into the ballroom, where the band had struck up a jazzy version of "Let it Snow." Mila excused herself to go to the restroom, leaving Max to track down some drinks. She wouldn't disappear for long.

When she entered the ladies' room, Lexy stood at the mirror, applying a layer of red lipstick, her lips forming a perfect pucker. Mila gave her a quick nod and averted her eyes, trying to avoid a conversation. Too much history had passed between them, and the tension thrummed like a bass guitar string.

Lexy swiveled around. "You look like you're enjoying the evening."

"Yes, I am." Mila tried to move forward, but Lexy blocked the way.

Lexy narrowed her eyes. "You know, before you came back to Wild Harbor, there was a history between Max and me."

Mila didn't want to have this conversation. Not now. Not ever. "The history between you and me goes back even further. Maybe it's time we just let it go."

"You want me to let Max go? You might have to ask him to do that. He was the one who pursued me."

"That's not what he told me. He's been avoiding you since I arrived home. Why do you think he asked me out?"

Lexy threw her head back and laughed. "How little you know about Max Malone. Has he shared his past? His family? Or hasn't he told you yet?"

A twinge of jealousy twisted inside Mila's stomach. How could he tell Lexy and not her? Lexy turned back to the mirror to finish her lipstick. "He's not interested in a relationship. Not after what happened in his family."

Mila lifted her chin. She didn't know the story, but she didn't believe Max would hurt her. "His feelings have changed."

"Has he told you about how his last girlfriend is dating his brother? That's why he can't move on. He's not the type who wants a long-term relationship, honey."

Mila shifted in her boots. It was true he hadn't said anything about their future together, and Mila hadn't wanted to rush things until she figured out her own feelings. But Lexy had slowly woven a thread of doubt under Mila's skin.

"It's none of your business what he tells me," Mila shot back.

"Why don't you ask him what he confessed to me on our date?"

"I don't need to know."

"Then prove me wrong. Ask him." Lexy leaned toward Mila, a hint of defiance in her eyes.

Mila brushed past her and locked herself in a stall. She heard Lexy's stilettos clicking across the tile floor, fading with the close of the bathroom door. She heaved a sigh of relief.

When she came out of the bathroom, she searched for Max in the dim light. That's when she spied him, tucked away in a corner with Lexy. Mila wove through the crowd as Lexy whispered something in his ear. Max laughed, then she touched his arm.

Step away, Mila silently pleaded, but he didn't move.

Mila halted in the middle of the crowd. Maybe Lexy was right. How could she not see it before?

Max glanced up, and his eyes locked with Mila's. Something passed across Max's face, an urgency that she didn't want to uncover.

She needed to leave before he humiliated her more. She took a few steps backward and bumped into a server carrying a dozen slices of cheesecake. The tray clattered to the ground, knocking desserts everywhere.

"I'm sorry," Mila said, before fleeing the room as quickly as possible.

"Mila!"

Max's voice fueled her step as she wove through the crowd,

racing to the foyer, where she began a full sprint out the doors. The last thing she wanted was to face him. Embarrassment drove her forward, the same way it had on the day of her wedding, when the entire church had been packed.

Now here she was again, saddled with the same weight of shame as she sprinted toward her car. The landscape was still as beautiful as she remembered when she'd stood on the balcony kissing Max. But this time she wanted to curse its beauty, like it had tricked her into believing she could love again.

"Mila, wait!" Max's voice erupted behind her as she reached her car.

Fumbling for her keys, she dropped her clutch on the ground and the contents spilled out. Mila fell to her knees, gathering her things when Max caught up.

"Why are you leaving? Is it because of Lexy?" He was breathing hard, confusion etched into his brow.

"Isn't it obvious?"

"What are you talking about? I was having the best evening of my life with you. Then you ran out on me."

"She told me about your brother's girlfriend. Then she said you confessed feelings for her."

Max paused.

Mila jumped on his hesitation. "So, it's true?"

"It's not like it sounds," he pleaded. "Let me explain."

"I can't do this now." She opened the door to her car and climbed in.

He wedged himself closer to keep her from shutting the door. "Where are you going?"

She started the car. "Home. I'm done. I'm tired of fighting this. You can have her."

"Mila, I don't want Lexy. I want *you.*"

"But this will never work. Can't you see that?"

"Give me one reason why this wouldn't work."

Tears formed in the corners of her eyes. She turned her face away, afraid of letting him see the emotion that was threatening to overwhelm her. "I don't know if I can trust someone again."

"When will you stop being afraid? I want to be with you. Isn't that enough?"

Mila gripped the steering wheel, her voice hard as stone. "Not anymore. I'm sorry, Max."

As she pulled away from him, she caught his figure in the rearview mirror, his hands hanging helplessly at his sides. She could barely make out his words as her engine roared out of the parking lot.

"Don't leave. Please."

But Mila was already gone, speeding through the night, toward an unknown future ahead.

CHAPTER FOURTEEN

MAX

Max stood in his kitchen, nervously looking at his phone. He had tried calling and texting Mila a dozen times, but she was clearly avoiding him. After several days, Max couldn't wait any longer. It was Christmas Eve, and he wanted to talk with her.

When he pulled up to her house, her car was gone. Not a good sign.

"Max, hello." Hesitation colored Diane's usual tone.

His eyes scanned the foyer in search of Mila. "Is Mila home?"

On the day before Christmas, Mila usually spent time with family cooking food and wrapping gifts, but now, the house seemed strangely silent.

"Mila isn't here. She left early this morning. She wouldn't tell us where she was going." A slow sadness stretched across Diane's face.

"Do you know what time she'll be back? I can wait."

Diane shook her head. "I wish I knew. I don't know what

happened, but I'm not sure Mila is coming back. She packed all her things."

"She went back to Chicago?"

Diane leaned against the door for support as if the weight of this news was exhausting. "It appears that way."

"I didn't think she'd leave without saying goodbye." Max felt like someone had socked him. "If you talk to her, would you tell her I'm trying to reach her?"

Diane pressed her lips into a melancholy smile and nodded. "I'm sorry, Max. I wish I had more information."

He turned and then remembered one more thing he wanted to tell Diane. "When I moved here, I didn't think I needed anyone. But you've made me feel like part of your family. I didn't realize how much I needed that."

Diane's expression melted into relief as she opened her arms to Max. "No matter how things turn out, you're always welcome here."

As she closed the door behind him, Max stood on the porch for a few seconds, his heart spiraling, like he had lost his footing. This wasn't how things were supposed to end. He had planned on spending Christmas Eve with Mila, not chasing her down and fixing the cracks in their relationship.

His phone buzzed as a picture appeared from his brother. Caleb stood next to his dad's bed, where his father lay, his gaunt face attempting a smile. On the other side of the bed was his mom. They were together, and he was the missing piece.

Caleb: Mom is only here for a short time. Sorry to miss you this Christmas. It might be Dad's final one. Dad and Mom send their love. Merry Christmas, brother.

For years, Mom had avoided Dad, blaming him for their child's accident and igniting a palpable tension between them. Her devastating grief had trickled into the cracks of Max's heart, filling it with resentment. If his sister hadn't died, his parents would still be together. His dad's mistake destroyed their family. Max couldn't forgive his father any more than his mother could.

He had inflicted his father with a lifetime of shame and regret. His dad had paid the price. But Max's absence demanded more.

What had brought Mom to his father's bedside now? It could only be one thing. The same thing Max needed to do. The one thing he could not give.

Forgiveness. Max had rationalized his own lack of compassion by pointing out his dad's failures. This bitter seed had rooted in his heart, convincing him he was justified in making his dad pay the price.

But the image of his mom next to his dad broke the thorny vine that had wrapped itself around Max's heart. It split his anger apart like an ax-head to a stump. The tendrils that had invaded every part of him were finally breaking, like an invasive vine being destroyed.

As Max sat in that space, the place where sorrow and forgiveness meet, he finally knew what he must do. It wasn't Mila he had to see. It was his father.

Two words would change everything: *I'm coming.*

MAX'S FATHER lived on the corner of the highway between a gas station and an abandoned house. The paint was badly peeling and the bushes outside were so overgrown they covered his windows, blocking the light. It looked like the home of a serial killer or the type of house kids avoided on Halloween.

The embarrassment of his childhood home nearly strangled Max. It was the same reason he had never brought friends home from school. He was from the wrong side of the tracks. Too poor to afford new clothes. Too embarrassed about their shabby property. He didn't want to be target practice for their cruel remarks.

When Max stepped onto the cracked porch stoop, he noticed the holes left in the cement where the iron railing had been. Max guessed it was falling off before his brother had ripped it out for good. This entire house was crumbling, decaying piece by piece.

The faded blue door was covered with a permanent layer of dust. He wanted to trace the words *wash me* across it. He swiped the dust with his fingertip, one long streak across the surface. Evidence he had returned. There was no turning back now.

The door swung open before he knocked. His brother stood in the opening, blinking back the light, tiny fault lines stretching from the corners of his eyes.

"Max." His eyes adjusted, but he still didn't smile. His face was filled with wonder and confusion, like Max was the shadow of a memory.

"How did you know I was here?"

"Dad saw a movement out the window. He thought it was the mailman." Caleb stepped back to let Max into the entry. "He's going to be so surprised."

Max put his hands in his coat pockets, his feet stuck to the decaying rubber mat. "Am I still invited?" His voice cracked. "It's been a long time, and I haven't exactly been nice to you."

Something flickered on his brother's face. "I know. I might have to beat you up for it later." His mouth jerked up at the corner. "You're still my little brother. Pretty sure I can still take you down."

The tension between them was shifting. For all his faults, Caleb had never held a grudge long.

"Who's here?" his mother's voice chimed in the background.

As Max stepped into the house, the scent of pine mixed with the faint smell of wood smoke and Old Spice overwhelmed him.

It was the scent of his boyhood. His mind spiraled back to snuggling with his father on camping trips and hiking in the summer rain, of stacking chopped wood and staring at the dusting of stars while the cicadas hummed.

Max's eyes adjusted to the dim light. The curtains were partially closed, and only one lamp glowed, a single bulb casting a halo of golden light on the floor.

"Max, you came." His mother stood to greet him and wrapped Max in a hug. It had been so long since he had seen her. As she pressed into him, her five-foot frame seemed so tiny against his own. Since when had she become so frail?

He scanned the living room, settling on his father. His dad lay on a medical bed, his pale face hollow, the shadows deepening in his cheekbones. His eyes flickered with light when he saw his son.

"Max." His father's voice came out in a raspy whisper, as if forming one word consumed his energy. He lifted his hand to Max, an invitation to step closer.

What do you say to someone who has hurt you so much that the scars still ached? Seeing his dad stripped of life, reduced to an invalid, turned something inside him, like a key opening a locked door. Maybe hope was possible.

Max took his father's palm in his, a once firm grip reduced to skin on bones. "It's been a long time."

Even though his breathing was labored, his father's eyes glittered in the dim light. "Too long. Please stay awhile."

Max sat next to his father as everyone looked on with wonder, as if they could hardly believe he had returned.

"Can I get you something?" His mom rubbed her hands together. "A glass of water?" She nervously glanced between father and son. Something had shifted with his mom. Max sensed she wanted to make things right.

"One for each of us," his father coaxed. "Max, move closer so I can see you."

Max stepped closer to his father's bed as his mother wandered to the kitchen. In the hall entrance, Taylor appeared.

"Hi, Max." She leaned against the corner of the entrance, keeping her distance. "It was nice of you to come."

"Hey, Taylor." He had expected more of a reaction, but the flame he had once held for her had extinguished like a puff of smoke. Maybe it was because everything paled in light of his dad's situation.

As his brother moved closer to Taylor, Max didn't sense any of the jealousy he had felt before. Now that he wanted to be with Mila, it changed everything.

"I should have come sooner." Max glanced at his father, who was still marveling that he was there. "I'm sorry for waiting so long."

His mother set two glasses of water on the end table between them. Max's mouth was like dry sand. He grasped the cold glass and took a sip.

His dad exhaled a strenuous breath that sounded like he was breathing through a drinking straw. "I'm just glad you came."

His brother put his hands in his pockets and nodded toward a photo album that was open on the couch. "Mom brought pictures of when we were kids. Wait until you see the haircuts she inflicted on us."

Mom clicked her tongue as her hand swept across faded photographs.

"Now, no complaining. We didn't have money for haircuts back then." She sat on the couch and flipped through a few pages, then held up a picture of Max and Caleb dressed in checkered button-down shirts, their hair neatly slicked to their scalps.

"This was the Easter when you were three." Mom pointed to a picture where Max's bangs were chopped in a crooked slant.

"At least we were cute." Max's lips twitched. He didn't want his mom to feel bad. Their lack of money had been a constant source of tension in the family.

His dad shook a finger toward the photo album. "Show him that camping trip to the Upper Peninsula."

Mom shook her head, as if even recalling that trip was exhausting. "A flat tire on our way north. Raccoons got into our food. It rained the whole time. From the pictures, you wouldn't even know. You both look so happy."

She passed the photo album to Max. Two little boys posed outside a tent. Max was covered in dirt and holding a gigantic stick while Caleb flexed his nonexistent boyish muscles.

"I loved that trip." Max flipped a page. "We played in the stream and got lost on adventures in the forest. It was like the entire world was ours to conquer."

Caleb sat down on the arm of the chair next to Max and peered over his shoulder. "One of my favorite trips. Except that the raccoons ate all our chocolate chip cookies."

Dad let out a tiny *huh* that sounded like a laugh and a real-ization. "All this time, I thought that trip was ruined. You boys liked it, and I didn't even know."

"It wasn't ruined, Dad," Caleb reassured him. "We made the best of an unpleasant situation."

Max flipped the page. His baby sister's face covered the entire page.

"Well, there's our sweet Jenny." His dad's expression softened as he gazed at her baby cheeks.

"I haven't seen these pictures in so long." Max frowned at the pages, wishing he could remember the sound of her voice.

When he glanced at Dad, he could see tears in the corners of his eyes. He couldn't tell if they were tears of regret or tears of what might have been, but he was a shattered man, someone who'd been broken repeatedly until there was nothing left.

His dad's breath came out in tiny gasps. "I'm sorry for how I handled everything after Jenny's death. I wanted to bring my little girl back, and I treated everyone rotten. I hope someday you can forgive me." His whole countenance was weary, like everything had been pressed out until there was nothing left.

How could he blame his father for breaking under the weight of grief? His sister's death, the crumbling of their family, the separation between them—it all had been too much.

"I forgive you." The words felt like a sweet release, a freedom he had not known he needed. "You're not the only one who messed up. I made you carry too much."

"Max, you never needed my forgiveness. It was already yours."

His dad leaned forward and wrapped his arms around Max.

Bitterness had cost him years, but in one moment, forgiveness had erased everything.

CHAPTER FIFTEEN

Mila took a deep breath as she waited outside the door of the church for the annual Christmas Eve service. It was now or never. She couldn't hide outside on the steps all evening.

Mila snuck in the back door of the church and was greeted with the refrain of "O Come, O Come Emmanuel" echoing through the church. She peeked in the back, her eyes scanning the rows until she finally found her family. When she slid into their pew, her parents glanced over, surprised to see her after she'd bolted out the door early this morning. Mila lowered her head, staring at the old wood floor. Memories were etched into the shiny surface, marking a hundred years of Wild Harbor history. Families had wedded, borne children, and died, each generation repeating the cycle. Decades of brides had walked across these pine planks, including her mother, who, along with her father, had vowed to love *until death do us part*.

She was doing the right thing leaving town tonight, but all she could think of was that moment on the balcony. She had never been happier than when she had been in Max's arms.

Earlier that day, she had escaped an hour north to a secluded beach where she would be a stranger. She nestled into the sand for the day, sorting out her feelings under a chilly blue sky. No one would find her.

As she'd sat huddled under a blanket, snow had lightly dusted the sand. The beach always soothed her in a way that nothing else could, and Mila felt the pulsating tide wash over her weary emotions. She could learn to let go of Max, even though everything begged her to hang on.

Her feelings for Max were making her sick with nerves, which meant she had to come up with a plan. Mila would go back to Chicago tonight, but first, she would attend the Christmas Eve service with her family. It was the least she could offer them, since she was missing Christmas Day with her family. She couldn't risk Max showing up at her parents' house uninvited. It would be better to return to her empty apartment in the city. To move on, no matter what her heart felt.

Now here she was, sitting in a candlelit church, trying to make peace with her decision. Where was clarity when she needed it most? She ached to hear God drop an answer in her lap, to confirm her decision was the right one.

She listened as the pastor read about the birth of Christ. Images of Max interrupted her focus. What was he doing tonight? She toyed with the phone in her hands, tempted to turn it on to see if he had tried to reach her.

The quiet muffle of a door closed behind her. She shifted and spied Max standing in the back of the sanctuary, scanning the seats. She turned away from him quickly and sank down. What if he wasn't looking for a seat, but was looking for her?

She peeked back and his gaze found hers across the sanctuary. Mila faced the front, her eyes on the actors playing Mary and Joseph, who sat serenely staring into a tiny infant's face. If Mila hadn't sensed the panic rising, it might have been a wonderful moment. But she couldn't stay still. An urgency drove her on. *Go, now.*

She tapped her mother's leg. "I'm so sorry, but I have to leave," Mila whispered to her family.

"What, why?" Thelma frowned.

"We haven't even lit the Christmas Eve candles yet," Mom protested.

Their confused looks only made her escape more awkward as she crawled over their legs, ready to bolt out of the church. Luckily, her aisle of escape was on the far end of the sanctuary, opposite Max.

As she dashed out of the foyer of the church and swung open the front door, she nearly knocked over Joshua.

He took a step back, but seemed unfazed by her frantic escape. A wool hat covered his ears as he dug his hands into his coat pockets.

"Merry Christmas, Mila. Where are you off to this fine Christmas Eve?" The question was light and unassuming, but she knew Joshua wasn't a dummy. No one fled from a church without a reason.

Mila opened her mouth, but she couldn't seem to formulate an answer. He wouldn't judge her, but she couldn't confess the real reason.

"I have to go. I'm sorry," she said, her voice cracking.

"You look upset. Anything I can help with?"

"You can't fix this."

He nodded, his thin lips clamped neatly together. The longer he stood there, the more he seemed to read her thoughts. Her head ached.

He rubbed his gloved hands together. "How is the Christmas Eve service?"

"The service?" She had almost forgotten. It was nearly identical every year. "They're probably lighting candles now as they sing carols. My favorite part."

The thought of Max, with candlelight glowing on his face, made her want to turn around.

Something soft and sad passed across Joshua's face. "You know what I marvel at when I read the Christmas story? This baby came to earth to be rejected. That's what he chose—rejection. Isn't that a miracle too?"

Mila gripped the edge of her coat and pulled the collar around her neck. Was it getting colder outside? A shiver ran down her arms. She didn't understand why Joshua was telling her this. "I'm leaving tonight."

His eyes dropped to her coat pocket. "I suppose your grandmother always knew. That's why she left you something."

She hadn't noticed it, but sticking out of the flap of her wool coat was a card with her grams's swooping cursive writing. She ran her fingers over the envelope, a small lump clearly visible under the surface.

Grams must have suspected that she wouldn't stay, and it pained her to think of them gathering for Christmas dinner without her. She'd miss her family's laughter echoing through the home as beef roasted in the oven. Would anyone remember to set the fancy butter dish next to the homemade strawberry jam? The jellied berries always spread perfectly inside one of Grams's homemade rolls—sweet, sticky jam glistening on shiny china. All the wonders of home wrapped in a hot, buttered roll. She marveled at how her heart kept beating this strong and steady when she was giving up so much.

Instead, she'd chosen to spend Christmas in her empty apartment like a faded half-person. Nothing was worse than a Christmas alone.

"I'm not feeling great. I'm sorry, Joshua." Her body was wrung out, and her head throbbed painfully. She'd never known how sick grief could make her.

"You haven't done anything wrong." He offered a warm

smile that felt like sunshine across her shoulders, the way a beam of light presses through a window on a chilly day.

Her throat ached like it was pricked with needles. "It seems I've done everything wrong. My shop. My life." She backed away from him and rubbed her fingers against her aching temples. Her world spun and tilted as her vision blurred for a second. Her body was revolting against the cold, and she wondered if she looked as bad as she felt. "I should get on the road."

Joshua's face melted into concern. "You don't look well. Can I help you?"

"I'm fine." She took a few more steps backward, wanting to sink down into a chair or a bed, anywhere she could rest. She needed to make it to her car before her resolve burned out and she crashed at her parents' house.

"Are you sure?" He reached toward her, but she held up her hand.

"Thank you, but no. I need to do this on my own." Then she turned and headed to her car, her wobbly legs threatening to collapse under her. A strange pain radiated from her bones.

Tears streamed down her neck as she climbed into her car. She didn't have to glance in her rearview mirror to know her mascara was leaving black streaks down her cheeks. A sad clown with painted tears. She placed her fingers on her temples and pressed the hollow spot where they throbbed.

As much as she tried to convince herself her relationship with Max was over, she didn't want it to be. In a perfect world, they'd be sharing this evening together, ending with a goodbye kiss on the front stoop of her house.

The image felt like shattered glass fanned across the floor. What she needed was to strangle these feelings until they suffocated and say goodbye to all the dreams she'd once had for them. No lucky coin could change her life. No magic snap of the finger. It was time to sever all ties to Max.

As she sped out of town, her throat burning, she could no longer think straight. Everything in her was numb, except for the hot pain radiating through her body. All she wanted now was to fall into her bed and not wake until the pain was gone.

SHE HAD no idea what time it was when she woke sprawled across her bed. She lifted her head and saw that she still wore her clothes from Christmas Eve. She brushed wisps of hair off her sweaty forehead and felt her blouse clinging to her wet back. Heat radiated through her body, even though she shook with chills. She tried to sit up, and pain shot through her skull like a bullet, making the room swirl.

"Ow," she moaned and stumbled off the bed and slipped to her knees.

Her body met the cool wood floor. She pressed her face to the smooth surface, and a tiny sensation of relief met her flaming cheek. She was sick on Christmas of all days. As if her life could get any worse.

She tilted her head toward the bathroom door and crawled, determined to locate a bottle of pain reliever. At least there was no one to see her in this miserable state.

"What are you doing up?" Max stood at the entrance of her room, staring down at her pathetic figure on the floor.

She squinted as her eyes adjusted to the dark. "How did you get in here?" She rubbed the massive pain in her forehead. It was awful, like a tire had run over her skull.

"Your sister has a key, remember?"

She had forgotten about the emergency key she'd given to Sophie when she moved to Chicago. Her sister had never bothered using it before.

"Why did she give it to you? I didn't ask you to come." Her words came out harsher than she'd meant them to, but she had no filter when she felt this horrible. Her body was like a wasted shell.

"You didn't ask, but Joshua did. He was concerned about you after you fled the church."

She slumped back against her bed. "He should have sent someone from my family."

She couldn't see Max's face clearly, but the words were like grenades lobbed in the dark.

"It's late, and your family's Christmas is in the morning, so he asked me to check on you. I couldn't leave you sick on the holiday."

She had no idea what time it was, but the world was black and silent. "I was already going to be alone on Christmas. I can take care of myself. Go enjoy your holiday."

With Lexy. She couldn't bring herself to say it, because everything in her body already ached too much. Did Lexy know where Max was right now? She'd follow after him and steal him away if she were his love interest.

"Is that why you were crawling on the floor?" She couldn't see his smile, but the way he said it hinted at one.

He stooped down and ran his fingers across her forehead. "You're burning up. Tell me where you keep the medicine."

"I'm perfectly fine to get it myself." She tried to stand, turning and grasping the footboard for support, but her legs wobbled under her. Max grabbed at her waist and seated her on the bed, like a rag doll.

"You are not fine. You're a furnace. If you refuse to tell me, I'll search for it myself." He went into her bathroom and started opening drawers. Embarrassment twisted inside as he searched her private drawers.

She couldn't take him rattling through her cupboards anymore. "It's in the cupboard over the toilet."

He approached her with two pills and a glass of water and sat on the edge of the bed. "Here, take this."

She gulped the pills down and then curled up in a fetal position. Her teeth chattered as she buried her face in a blanket. "I'm . . . so . . . cold."

"Do you want to change your clothes?" He stroked her hair. "You look . . . well, no offense, but you look rather uncomfortable in a blouse and skirt."

It was true she was miserable, but she could hardly move. She moaned in response.

"Why don't I find some pajamas for you? I'm sorry, but I can't help you with . . ." He circled his fingers toward her clothes.

"I feel like I'm dying." She closed her eyes.

A dresser drawer slid open and then shut.

"Uh, so there's this." He held up a pair of flannel pajamas with llamas on them. "Or this?" The other option was a T-shirt-and-shorts set with Christmas cats.

"Llamas or cats?"

"Llamas." She frowned. "Please don't make fun of me for this later."

He laid the llama pajamas next to her. "I won't. But I won't forget either."

He patted her shoulder and left the room.

She stripped off her skirt and unbuttoned her blouse. Her body shivered as she dragged her tired legs into the pants and fumbled at the buttons on the shirt. She didn't even care if she put on her pajamas correctly. She flopped back on the bed, her body riddled with exhaustion. If she had more energy, she would have said goodbye to Max before he left, but she was too weary to make it across her apartment. Would she even remember he had been here? She wasn't sure. Huddling under the blankets, her eyes drifted shut like a black curtain descending on a theater. As her mind spiraled into darkness, all she could think was that he had come. *For her.*

When she woke, the sunlight drifted through a crack in her

curtain. A long yellow ray sprayed her eyelids with light. She rolled over and buried her nose in the pillow, her body wet with sweat. She had to escape from these blankets before she suffocated.

Tossing the comforter off, she lifted her head and blinked back the blinding light. Her head still ached painfully, but her body was no longer shaking with cold.

She dragged herself to the bathroom and searched through the cabinet for a thermometer. It wasn't in its usual place, but she couldn't remember moving it.

In the mirror, she glimpsed her face and was shocked by how bad she looked. A grey pallor had settled over her colorless skin, like the ground turkey meat that had spoiled in her fridge. Her hair was damp from sweat and smashed on one side, and her pajama top was buttoned crookedly, leaving a mismatched, gaping neckline. Every time she blinked, the heat from her head cooked the back of her eyes.

She dragged her weary body to the kitchen.

"Good morning," a voice chimed.

Mila jerked around. Max stood by the coffee maker, his body resting against the edge of the counter.

What was he doing here? A watery memory floated to the surface of her brain. In her feverish fantasy, he had found her on the bedroom floor last night, but she couldn't remember much else. The flashback was like a strange dream, where he slowly evaporated like morning fog. But her eyes confirmed the truth: there was a live, gorgeous man in her apartment. Not just any man, but Max. Even in her sick state, her body wanted to curl up into his.

"I forgot you were here," her voice croaked. "I'm searching for the thermometer."

She opened her junk drawer and raked her hands through it.

Max pulled it out of his back pocket and held it in front of her.

"You had it?" She put out her hand, briefly annoyed that he had searched her cabinets. Her emotions felt chiseled by a dull saw, edgy and ragged. "I want to make sure my fever is gone."

"Your temperature two hours ago was still 102. But at least it had dropped from 104." He checked his watch. "Time to take your pills again."

"You took my temperature while I slept?" She stuck the thermometer under her armpit as she leaned against the kitchen counter and narrowed her eyes. She couldn't remember him coming last night or taking her temperature.

"I placed it under your arm. Nothing more." His eyes swept over the crooked collar of her shirt.

"You know I was sick last night when I buttoned this." She frowned at him.

He lifted his hands in the air. "You don't have to explain. I can see how sick you are."

"Were."

"Are," he countered. "You still *are*."

"Were. I woke up blazing hot. My fever broke last night."

"We'll see." He seemed sure of himself. How did he even know? He wasn't a doctor, and she was feeling loads better.

The thermometer beeped. She glanced down. 101.5. Still sick.

"Well?" He lifted his eyebrows.

"I'm fine." She hid the thermometer behind her back.

"I'm not leaving until you show me it's normal." He grabbed it out of her hands and his eyes flitted over the number. "Not normal yet. That means I stay."

"Max, I'm fine."

"You look like death."

"Gee, thanks. How about now?" She crossed her eyes and let her tongue hang out.

"You're weird when you're sick." A grin spread across his

face. "Take your pills." He shoved two more pain relievers her way and a glass of water. "Merry Christmas."

Her eyes widened. "It's Christmas?" She smacked her forehead. "I totally forgot. You can't be here. You need to go home." She grabbed his arm and shoved him toward the door, but he was massively strong, a pillar of unmovable stone. Her feet skated out from under her on the tile floor.

"In your state, you shouldn't be alone." His eyes locked on hers.

A fluttery feeling rose in her stomach. Apparently having a fever didn't squelch her reaction to him.

"Thank you for your offer, but I don't need help. Plus, it's Christmas, and you shouldn't be here."

She retreated to her bedroom, shutting the door and falling onto the bed. She wasn't a baby and didn't need his assistance, even though a tiny piece of her didn't mind having him in her apartment.

She snuggled under the blankets, her head sinking into the pillow, her eyelids heavy. At one point, she felt fingertips slip across her cheek, a palm flattening against it, then a wet rag dragged over her forehead. Later, fingers stroked her head, and a voice whispered something in her ear.

In a muddled state between waking and sleep, she couldn't understand it. Confused thoughts spiraled through her mind, like a hawk making lazy loops in the sky. Her dry lips formed soundless words. As her body blazed with heat, she dreamed of fire, a circle of flaming light. A hand touched her forehead, then moved her body, folding her into someone's arms. Cradled there, her cheek pressed into a baby-soft T-shirt. Every part of her ached.

When she woke, her eyelids fluttered open, the memory of being held long gone. The sunlight had faded into darkness as the room took shape. Dresser, bed, curtains. No more spinning walls. Twisting her legs over the bed, she knocked into someone's shoulder.

"Easy, killer." Max stood up and placed his hands on her shoulders, blocking her from getting out of bed.

"What are you doing on my floor? I thought you'd left by now." Her words were sharp. She was tired of running into him without warning.

"You were still sick. Your fever spiked again. Who would make you take your medicine if I left?"

"I would."

He looked doubtful.

She rubbed her head. "Okay, maybe not. But I feel a little better. And hungry. What time is it?" Her stomach felt like a sad, empty little pit.

"It's six o'clock."

"In the evening? I can't believe I slept all day. I missed Christmas."

"You didn't. It's still Christmas. Let's take your temperature."

She flopped back onto her pillow and stuck the thermometer under her arm as she looked at the crack on her ceiling. It stretched the entire length of her bed, like a winding road on a map that led to nowhere. The device under her arm beeped. 97.3.

"It's normal!" She waved the thermometer toward him to prove it. "I've been dreaming of pot roast and mashed potatoes with bread. No, scratch the bread. I want rolls with real butter and strawberry jam."

"Could you be more specific?" He gave her a wry smile while he searched his phone for a restaurant. "Do you know how hard it is to find a restaurant open on Christmas Day? Much less that exact menu?"

"Probably next to impossible."

"I'll see what I can do. You rest." A wave of homesickness hit her stomach. If she had stayed in Wild Harbor, she could be recovering in her childhood room while her mom carried up Christmas dinner on a TV tray, just like when she was little.

Instead, she was relying on this incredibly generous man to take care of her, who was off-limits now that she had seen how he looked at Lexy. Her heart swung like a pendulum in her chest between *I love him, I love him not.*

Her voice stuck in her throat, strangling her from asking him why he was here when he could be with someone else. Vulnerable conversations weren't her forte, and her heart was worn out from hoping for too much. She needed to learn to live with rejection.

As he dashed out of the apartment in search of food, she stripped off the llama pajamas and hopped into the shower, hoping she could wash her feelings down the drain. Cranking the water until the bathroom mirror fogged, she stood under the shower and let the water dissolve her sweat and tears. She couldn't think about Max Malone like she used to anymore.

When her skin was wrinkled and pink, she changed into a knit dress tasteful enough for Christmas, but as soft as a baby's T-shirt. Like Max's shirt. Why did everything circle back to him?

When Max returned, his eyes flitted over her. He looked both pleased and confused. "You heading out?"

"After all that sweat, I was the grossest human being ever. I thought you deserved something better."

"You looked good before, Mila. You always do."

The way he said it made her heart trip over its normal rhythm. If a man could see you at your worst and still say you looked good, it was proof he was a keeper. But in this case, not hers to keep.

"I brought food." He pulled out a container of roast beef and mashed potatoes. "You're lucky the diner was open. They even had rolls."

"And strawberry jam?"

"Well," he said, pausing for effect. He kept her hanging by a thread. "Not homemade. I had to pull some strings for that."

He lifted what looked like a pint of fresh strawberry jam.

Her eyes widened. "Where did you find that bottle of goodness?" She wanted to take a spoon and eat it straight from the container.

"Secrets. Don't ask." He popped the lid open and held the jam to her nose before carrying it to the table. All her reluctance toward him was dissolving like snow on a sunny sidewalk. She wouldn't trample into uncomfortable questions about his relationship with Lexy. For now, she'd enjoy her dinner.

Merry Christmas to me.

He picked up the Christmas candle from the island and transferred it to the table, lighting it between them. The fire caught his blue eyes, dark sapphires glittering in the light, while the window framed a snow-globe scene. Everything she had ever wanted, but nothing she could have. Not beyond today.

After being sick, Mila couldn't believe how delicious everything tasted. She wanted to gorge herself, especially on rolls and jam.

"Save room for dessert," Max warned her.

"You bought dessert? I didn't ask for it."

"But I knew you'd want it."

She licked the spoon from the jam jar. "This was like dessert for me. I'm not sure anything could top it."

"How about a coffee?" He tossed his napkin on the table and headed to the kitchen. She followed, leaning across the island as he worked his magic.

"You have a sad coffee maker," he teased.

"Spoken like a true barista."

"Which is why I'm not using it. I have an emergency French press in my car." He held up the small glass pitcher.

"Fancy and appropriate, given you own a café."

He set his phone next to her. "Can you set the timer when I'm ready? Essential for the correct brew."

"Of course." Like she knew anything about making coffee with a French press. The only thing she knew about coffee was how to order one.

He measured the grounds for the French press and boiled water.

"What's for dessert?"

"My options were limited, given it's Christmas. But there was this little bakery down the road that I found."

He opened a box which held an entire cheesecake decorated with fresh strawberries and drizzled with chocolate.

"You bought the whole thing? Max, I can't eat that."

"I know. That's why I'm here. To help you finish it."

Was he trying to ruin her waistline? She didn't know, and she didn't care. Deep red strawberries fanned across the cake. Cheesecake was the one dessert she had always requested for her birthdays growing up. Not classic white birthday cake. Not chocolate cupcakes. He was a mind reader, and she was falling under his spell, one delicious bite at a time.

"You know how to win my heart, Max Malone." The words spilled out before she could stop them.

"That's the idea," he shot back before turning to the French press. "Start the timer for four minutes. Then I'll cut the dessert." He sliced the cake into neat little triangles and slid them onto plain red dessert plates. With the white cheesecake and red strawberries on top, the scene begged for a photo shoot. The timer dinged as he finished preparing the coffee.

"Oh, I almost forgot your gift." He spun on his heel.

"What gift?"

Max pulled out a wrapped box with a red bow. "While you were sleeping today, I went out and bought this." He slid the gift in front of her. "Go ahead. Open it."

She rotated the beautifully wrapped gift in her hands. Guilt was overwhelming her. "Max, I don't have a gift for you."

"That's okay. It's a small present I stumbled on at one of the stores . . . and, well, I couldn't stop myself."

She unwrapped the paper and opened the box. "A mug?" When she pulled it out, it had a llama decked out in a Christmas hat that read "Fa la la llama."

She smiled. "In honor of my pajamas?"

He nodded. "I promised not to tease you, but I never promised not to bring it up again." He took the mug, rinsed it, then poured the coffee. A plate of cheesecake slid her way.

She took a slow bite of the dessert as he watched her.

"How is it?" His eyes were on her lips.

"So good I could cry." She savored the next bite of a huge strawberry, then realized her terrible manners.

He laughed. "I'm so glad you like it."

They ate their desserts, then pushed their plates aside and lingered over coffee until it was late.

Max's expression suddenly grew serious. "I finally had a talk with my family. If I couldn't even talk with you about it, I knew I had a problem."

"Oh? How'd it go?" She sat up straighter, not wanting to push him.

"Better than I thought. My dad and I finally had the conversation we've been needing to for the last decade."

"Was your brother there with Taylor?"

"He was, but it was different this time. I realized Taylor was never my perfect match." He looked like he was going to say more, but stopped.

"Really?"

"It was the strangest thing. I've been angry for so long, but when I saw my dad, it's like all the resentment disappeared. Poof. Up in smoke. I didn't want to live that way anymore."

"There's another reason you didn't want to live like that." Mila touched Max's arm. "You're a good man."

"No. A good man would have reconciled a long time ago. But I'm glad I didn't wait anymore." His gaze drifted to her hand on his arm, then to her lips, a shadow darkening his face like clouds on a sunny day.

"I should go."

She wished he wouldn't, but she couldn't ask him to stay longer. He'd already done so much for her already. "You saved my Christmas. Otherwise, I would have moped around my apartment feeling sorry for myself."

"I know. That's why I came." His wry smile made her light up. He grabbed his coat and a few belongings, hesitating for a second as he glanced her way, one last moment of connection.

She couldn't keep him to herself. He'd been at her apartment since Christmas Eve. Surely Lexy was wondering where he was.

She spotted his phone on the island and hurried to grab it before he left. A message flashed across the screen. Even though she knew she shouldn't read it, curiosity overwhelmed her.

Lexy: Merry Christmas, Max. Let's get together soon. Much love.

Emojis of hearts and red lips were stamped across the screen. Pain twisted through her as she turned the phone over, sickened by the words. Max was putting on his coat, oblivious to how she was crumbling inside.

"Here's your phone." She slid the phone into his coat pocket, hiding the ugly feeling rising inside her. She wanted to reply, *Stop contacting me,* then block her texts. Lexy brought out all kinds of monstrous thoughts in Mila, especially when it came to Max. She needed to do better.

"Goodbye, Max. Thank you for coming." She hoped he didn't

notice her abruptness, like her words were clipped too close around the edges.

Something flickered across his face. "Are you trying to get rid of me?" he teased.

She shook her head. Of course she was, if only to numb the pain. As nice as the evening had been, there was still so much that wasn't resolved between them.

"You've spent a lot of time here." She drew her arms around herself and leaned against the wall. "I'm grateful you came, but you should get back."

He hesitated, then took a step forward. He tilted her chin toward him softly. He was going to kiss her. She could see it in his eyes.

He moved his face close to her. Eye to eye. Breath to breath. His eyelids closed as she turned her face away. She couldn't kiss him now.

Almost like a whisper, his lips brushed her cheek with the lightest touch. A goodbye that left her aching for more.

Her heart was yo-yoing between wanting to push him away and pulling him back to her.

His eyes searched hers, confusion spinning like orbiting planets between them.

"Merry Christmas, Mila."

"Merry Christmas," she whispered.

"When will I see you again?"

She shrugged. "I have to catch up on work before the end of the year." Work was her go-to excuse for avoiding Max now. He was a business owner and knew the sacrifices.

He nodded, unconvinced. "But not New Year's Eve."

"We'll see."

"I'm not allowing you to ring in the new year alone. Trust me on this."

Could she? She nodded, even though she still had doubts.

He brushed her cheek. "I'll track you down before I let you sit in your apartment by yourself."

"Oh, really?" Every cell went on high alert in response to his touch. She felt radioactive. "I'll let you know." A vague answer was so much easier to hide behind.

As she shut the door behind him, she leaned against it and slid to the floor, her head in her hands.

Love wasn't supposed to be this complicated. There was no way she would compete with Lexy. Either she needed to step away from this relationship forever or force herself to have a heart-to-heart with Max. No more playing games.

A small, white triangle edge peeked out of her coat pocket. *Grams's card.*

She grabbed the envelope and ripped it in one clean line. The check fluttered from the card onto the floor as Mila pulled out a silver coin, one just like Gramps used to tuck into her Christmas cards every year.

She smoothed her thumb over the coin, feeling the outline of cold metal under her fingertips.

Mila,

Max told me the story of your fake date arrangement and my first reaction is that you'd fooled old Grams at her own game. Despite knowing this, I'm giving you a check to help with your shop. No strings attached. You fulfilled your end of the bargain, and I want to help. You can't talk me out of it, so don't even try.

Max melted this stodgy old lady's heart by admitting he had fallen for you. He's probably not going to tell you because he's a respectful gentleman. But I like him. He's a good one. Worth taking the risk, if you're willing to do the same.

I'm not much for sentiment, but Gramps always liked giving you these silver dollars. I could tell you it's a lucky coin, but I

don't want to lie, and you don't need luck, anyway. Your gramps would be so proud. He was the one who taught me that everything worth having is worth the risk.
Love,
Grams

Mila opened the check and gasped at the amount. Grams had given her more than she needed to cover her bills and expenses. Mila folded the check carefully and placed it on the table, her eyes pricked with tears. It was too generous to keep, but her grams wouldn't let her give it back. It would be an insult to turn it away.

Mila turned the coin around in her fingers. It was identical to the silver dollar she had given away on that bitterly cold evening before her entire life had changed. The day she'd met Max.

She shoved the coin into her wallet, burying it deep. It was time to make some hard decisions.

First, she needed to do something about the wedding dress. It hung in the closet, mocking her, representing all she had once dreamed of before her life had fallen apart.

She couldn't stand the memory of her failed engagement anymore.

Running to the closet, she swung open the doors and tore at the dress until it fell from the hanger and crumpled onto the floor.

She wanted the dress gone. To finally bury the past so she could move on.

Only one person knew she still had the wedding gown in her closet. *Cassidy.* Her friend would help her get rid of it for good.

She picked up her phone and rehearsed the words that would finally release her from the past.

"Cassidy, I'm ready to get rid of the dress."

CHAPTER SIXTEEN

MAX

Max couldn't put his finger on what had been wrong when he'd left Mila's place, but something had clearly shifted. He could see it in her eyes when he'd tried to kiss her lips. Hesitation had replaced longing.

The week between Christmas and New Year's stretched painfully on. The café stayed busy with its usual holiday clientele. Still, he waited for some response from Mila. A sign that she'd be coming home for New Year's Eve. He sent one last text before closing, hoping she might say yes.

Max: What are you doing for New Year's Eve? The invitation for tonight is still open. Don't make me track you down.

He would find her if she didn't respond. She couldn't hide from him forever. He glanced at the clock. Five minutes until closing.

The café was shutting down earlier than normal so he could attend the New Year's Eve countdown party in front of the clock tower. But now his plans were up in the air. He'd even drive to Chicago and wait by her door if that was what he needed to do.

He wiped down the last table, oblivious to the fact that one last customer had entered while his back was turned.

"You never responded to my message," Lexy murmured behind him.

He swiveled toward her. "Which one? We see each other all the time."

The look on her face was a mixture of annoyance and boredom. "The Christmas one."

"The one with all the heart and lip emojis?" He hadn't wanted to acknowledge that message for a reason. He shrugged. "I didn't think it needed a response."

"I thought there was something between us." She leaned against a nearby table, her body stretched tight like a rubber band. "At least that's how you felt once."

She hadn't forgotten the date, the one where he had mistakenly admitted he was interested in her. It had been a rash thought that had flitted through his mind for two seconds before he'd said it out loud and realized his blunder.

When he'd first moved to town, he'd been a lonely newcomer with a broken heart. Taylor had burned him, and Lexy was an attractive single woman. A terrible combination for someone who desperately needed to find his place. But after a few weeks, it became clear she wasn't his type. His feelings had changed, but somehow, she wouldn't let his comment go.

"When I said that, it was a mistake. I was lonely when I moved here," Max reminded her. "Didn't know a soul. I appreciated your friendship—the way you came alongside me when everyone was skeptical because I was a stranger. But face it, we're not a good match."

Lexy was a nice girl, but she didn't make his pulse race like Mila did.

"It's someone else, isn't it?" She frowned, clearly dissatisfied with his answer.

"Even if it wasn't, I couldn't be with you."

Her lips tightened. "Well, then. I guess my time here is over. Maybe it's time for you to find a new realtor for your investment properties." She swiveled on her heel and headed for the door.

"You're right. Consider yourself officially let go."

He'd find another realtor, but he couldn't find anyone like Mila.

A knock at the door interrupted her exit as Cassidy waved from the other side of the glass. He waved her in as Lexy brushed by her.

"Hi, Lexy," Cassidy chirped.

Lexy lifted a hand but didn't bother turning. Her face was as cold as a steel plate.

"Max, do you have any muffins left?" Cassidy's eyes drifted over to Lexy who stormed past the window of the café. "I'm sorry if I interrupted. I didn't know someone else was here."

Max cleared his throat. "You didn't interrupt anything. She was just leaving."

"Boy, she's in a mood."

"My fault." He threw a towel over his shoulder. "I was honest with her. Just fired her from being my realtor."

"Really? That's great news." Cass held her breath, like she was going to burst. "I'm not supposed to tell you this. But did you hear that Mila's home?"

"What? No. I texted her this week, and she hasn't responded. I've been trying to convince her to go to the New Year's Eve party tonight. I can't believe she didn't tell me she was coming." If she was trying to stay away from him, she was doing a good job of it.

"We're talking about Mila here. After Jake broke things off, it's like she lost all confidence in ever meeting a man who wouldn't disappoint her. Until a week ago, she hung on to her wedding gown. She finally asked me to get rid of it."

"Did you?"

Cassidy nodded.

No wonder she wouldn't let him into her life.

"What should I do?"

Cassidy shrugged. She seemed as confused as he was. "Max, I've known Mila all my life. When she's scared, she runs away. It's always how she's been."

"What do I do about it?"

Cassidy grabbed his arm and pulled him toward the door. "Don't let her get away this time."

WHEN MAX SHOWED up at Mila's house, his confidence had slipped a few notches. He'd hatched a plan, but now it seemed so ridiculous, he wasn't even sure if he'd be brave enough to go through with it. According to Cassidy, everyone from the family was gone for the evening, leaving Max the perfect opportunity to get Mila's attention.

The light from her bedroom glowed dimly through a curtain. He eyed the height of the roof on the back porch and shook his head. There was no way he could jump high enough to reach it. He turned and spied their old shed, where he hoped her dad kept a ladder. He prayed Brian had left it unlocked. As he tried the handle, the door clicked open and Max spied a ladder just the right height for climbing the porch roof where he could reach her window.

This was crazy, but he didn't care anymore.

He climbed the ladder, then scaled the porch roof, not expecting how difficult this would be when he couldn't see his footing clearly. He took a step forward and tripped on a fallen twig, which caused him to lose his balance and knock against the house with a thud.

The curtain shifted as Mila appeared, eyes wide. "Max?" The window creaked open. "What are you doing out there?" Her voice was a mixture of wonder and confusion.

"What does it look like?"

She shook her head. "You're going to get yourself killed falling off the porch roof. Why didn't you use the front door like a normal person?"

"Because I wanted to serenade you, like Romeo."

She blinked and stared at him. "But why?"

He needed to do this before he chickened out. "I meant it when I said I'd track you down, so here I am." He took a step closer to her window and grabbed the edge. He could finally see her eyes clearly, the moon reflecting across her cheek. "Now that I found you, would you go with me to the New Year's Eve party tonight?"

"I don't think it's a good idea."

He couldn't back down. Not now. "You haven't even given me a chance yet."

"No amount of persuasion is going to change my mind. It's clear there's something between you and Lexy. To compete with her would be ludicrous."

"I'm not interested in Lexy," he shot back.

"Then why does she send you emojis of hearts and lips? Why does she sign her texts with *much love?*"

"How did you . . . ?" He stopped, only just remembering when Lexy's text had come in. It was the night he had been at Mila's apartment.

She kept going before he could respond. "Then tonight, I was going to stop by the French Press, but when I pulled in, it was just you and Lexy together. I never got out of my car."

He didn't know she'd seen him tonight at the café. He'd been so close to her without even realizing it. "Just give me a chance to explain."

"I've tried, but every time I turn around, she's there. With you. I'm tired of feeling this way." She lowered the window, but Max reached forward to stop it. "You need to listen to me. Give me a chance to explain."

"It's too late." She tried to shut the window, but he wouldn't let her, so she turned away and left. He stood helplessly watching her as she walked out of her bedroom.

Then he remembered what Cassidy had mentioned. *She's a runner. The type to flee.* If she was having one of her freak-out-and-escape sessions now, he needed to stop her before she left.

He scrambled down the ladder and raced around the front of the house just in time to catch her before she made it to her car.

"Mila, don't do this again!" Max ran after her.

She jumped into the driver's side and started the engine. As she creeped forward, Max jumped in front of her vehicle, forcing her to slam on her brakes. Her car lurched to a stop, inches from his body.

"I won't let you leave this time," Max panted heavily from his sprint. He leaned forward, slamming his hands on the hood of her car. "You've already hit me once, you'll have to hit me again if you're going to leave."

Mila rolled down her window. "I need you to move, Max."

"I'm not moving until you agree to talk to me." His jaw was set.

She beeped her horn to force Max to move. "If you don't get out of the way, I'm going to have to hit you."

Max stood resolute and leaned closer to her windshield, speaking the words slowly. "Then hit me."

Mila paused, her hands gripping the steering wheel, white-knuckled.

"I can't." Her eyes beaded with tears. She tilted her head back to keep them from slipping down her cheeks.

He had called her bluff. She might run from him, but she'd never intentionally hurt him.

What he needed to do now was convince her of his love, or he'd lose her forever. "Mila, will you stop and listen to me? I don't want anyone else. I never have. I want you. I want *us*."

Something softened in her face. He was finally breaking through her walls.

She wiped her eyes and looked at her lap. "When I saw you and Lexy at the gala and the way you were looking at her, I thought I'd been a fool. How stupid was I to believe that you would choose me over her?"

"I don't have feelings for Lexy."

"She said you confessed it to her."

He sighed. "We went out on a few dates when I first moved here. For one foolish second, I blurted out that I was interested in her and then quickly regretted it. After spending time with her, I knew she was all wrong for me. But she wouldn't take no for an answer."

"What about tonight? When I saw you with her, it was like something broke in me. All the things from my past resurfaced, and I just wanted to run."

Jake had scarred her before, and he'd only added to her pain. "It was Lexy's last-ditch attempt to see if I was interested in being something more. I made it clear I wasn't. We're parting ways for good. Ask Cassidy. She was there when Lexy left."

Max wanted to move closer to Mila, but he was still afraid she would drive away. He held his ground, resolute, his face pleading for another chance. "You're running from fear. But I want you to trust me on this. Can you look at me?"

Her eyes slowly drifted toward his.

"As soon as I saw you bolt tonight, I knew what was happening. I was so afraid I'd never get to explain. I thought you'd never come back, and I'd never get the chance to tell you I'm falling in love with you." Max said it so simply, so softly. He didn't offer the words carelessly. "Mila, I choose *you*."

Without thinking, Mila took her foot off the brake, and the car lurched forward. Max jumped back just in time before Mila hit the brakes again.

"Oh, Max, I forgot to put the car in park. I'm so sorry!" She jumped out of the car and into his arms, her whole body melting into his. He picked her up off the ground, arms encircling her waist, spinning her in a slow, dizzying circle.

He caught his breath, adrenaline still surging through his body. "I never knew love would be so risky. Please don't hit me if I say it again." Max smiled and slid his hands around her waist as he lowered her to the ground.

"I promise I won't." Then she reached up, cupped his face in her hands, and kissed his lips. She angled into him as he wrapped his arms around her back, his fingers trailing up her spine. He leaned into the embrace, letting it take him away, and then drew her closer, unable to resist. He kissed her jaw, her cheekbones, and then his fingers stroked her nape. After a few seconds, she pulled away and leaned her forehead to his. Her breath sounded like she couldn't believe this moment was real.

"Max, you once said that confessing the truth makes a good plan B. So here goes nothing." She swallowed hard. "I'm falling in love with you. I tried to convince myself I wasn't. I pushed you away. And yet, you kept coming back for me."

He touched her nose with his fingertip. "I will always be there for you."

She hugged him harder. "I won't run away again."

His eyebrows shot up. "Promise?"

She nodded. "I promise."

"Does this mean you'll go with me to the party tonight?" He couldn't hide a smile as he wrapped her even tighter.

"As long as you don't mind spending it with me."

"I want to spend every New Year's Eve with you. I'd even get hit with your car again, if it would keep you in Wild Harbor."

"All you have to do to keep me in Wild Harbor is give me another kiss." Mila's smile was enough of an invitation. She didn't have to ask twice. In the distance, they could hear the clock tower bring in the new year and a crowd erupt in cheers.

Before she could say more, Max's lips were on hers, his hands sliding down her back. He didn't notice the snow that had started to fall around them. All he knew was how right it felt to hold her in his arms. This time, he'd never let her go.

CHAPTER SEVENTEEN

MAX

NEW YEAR'S DAY

Max's chest pounded like a racehorse as he approached his dad's place. He grabbed Mila's hand for support.

Before now, he would have felt the flush of shame as he showed her his shabby childhood home, but now, the embarrassment had worn off. She needed to see where he had come from without him covering up anything. He had shared all the ugly parts of his life with her, and she hadn't flinched once. If she could love him fully knowing about his past, then there would be no shame between them.

As they stepped into his dad's home, his mom welcomed Max and Mila with a hug. "You're both here. I was hoping you'd bring this young lady around before I left." Mom smiled, and the wrinkles around the edges of her eyes creased.

Taylor and Caleb stayed to the side, exchanging glances. Without hesitating, Mila stepped forward. "Hi, I'm Mila."

Caleb wrapped his arm around his girlfriend. "I'm Caleb, and this is Taylor." Taylor stepped forward with a bit of hesitation.

"I love your necklace." Mila admired the emerald hanging from Taylor's neck. After working with customers for years, she always seemed to know the right thing to say.

"Oh, thank you. It was a gift from Caleb."

"It's lovely." Mila smiled. "He has good taste."

It was all she needed to say before the two women connected. Taylor pulled Mila over to the side to talk about her wedding shop, while Max looked on in amazement. Relief drained from his body. He'd wanted this visit to go well, and thanks to Mila, it would.

"They seem to have hit it off." Caleb glanced wondrously at them.

Max shook his head. "I never would have imagined."

In the living room, his father erupted in a chest-rattling cough.

Max tugged on Mila's elbow gently. "Sorry to interrupt, but we have one more person to meet."

Taylor shook her head. "You know, Max, I never thought I'd instantly be taken with someone you brought home. But I can already see what a warm, lovely person Mila is."

Mila put her hand up in protest. "Max would tell you I haven't always been warm or lovely. My first response to him was to run away, but he's always persistently chased me down."

Caleb chuckled. "Someone to give him a run for his money? Then you're perfect."

His father's weary face lit up as soon as he spied Mila.

Max took her hand and led her toward his father. Holding her hand would never get old. "Dad, this is Mila, the girl I was telling you about." Max couldn't stop smiling. Just seeing his dad's approval filled him with a golden glow.

Mila's expression split wide open. "I didn't know you were talking about me with your family."

"All good, I promise. They were giving me relationship advice, actually." Max hoped she wouldn't press for details.

"Mila, finally," he wheezed as he took her hand and patted it. "Welcome to the family." He shifted to Max. "You didn't give up."

"I took your advice."

She wrapped her arm through his. "I didn't know your dad gave you advice."

Max put his cheek against her hair. "Father and son talk. His advice worked, and that's all that matters now. You're stuck with me." He kissed the top of her head.

"There's no one I'd rather be stuck with."

From the kitchen, his mother pulled out drawers as dishes clattered. "The roast is cooked and the potatoes are ready. Would someone put the rolls and jam on the table?"

"I'll help," Taylor called, then pulled Caleb along to join her.

Max squeezed Dad's hand. "Can we bring you a plate of food?"

"Sure. And put extra jam on my roll, okay?"

"You can't eat alone." Mila frowned and turned to Max. "Is it possible for us to eat here?"

"Why not?" Max shrugged as he headed toward the kitchen.

Mila wrapped her arm through his. "Is there a reason we're eating the exact same meal you brought me on Christmas?"

"I may have dropped a hint. Mom made the jam fresh this morning."

"What? You wooed me with that strawberry jam. My last defense fell when I ate that delicious spread."

"Then my plan worked." He nuzzled his nose in her hair before his lips dropped to her ear. "I saved the cheesecake for backup, in case the jam wasn't enough."

She leaned into him, and he wrapped his arm around her waist and gave it a squeeze.

"You've always been enough, Max Malone. Like a Christmas wish come true, even though I don't believe it's possible."

"What do you believe, then?" He stopped her in the hall before they reached the kitchen and swung her toward him.

"That every hard thing has led me to you, and it's better than I dreamed."

"Better than strawberry jam?"

She stood on her tiptoes and wrapped her arms around his neck, kissing his forehead. "Even better than that."

EPILOGUE

MILA

THE FOLLOWING SUMMER

As Mila stood outside the empty storefront on the corner of Main Street, she grabbed Max's hand.

"You honestly don't mind if I'm just down the street from the French Press?"

"Mila, I love that you're buying the old Baker storefront. It's a beautiful historic building. When the owner announced he was retiring, I knew it would be the perfect location to open your second shop."

Mila examined the large display windows and old brick detailing the exterior. She could already imagine the wedding dresses styled perfectly in the window, the lights gleaming off the delicate folds as women stopped to admire the antique-inspired lace or the hand-stitched beading.

So much had happened since Christmas. When she had returned to the city after the holidays, she and Max had agreed to see each other every weekend, as long as Hadley could cover the shop on Saturdays.

Instead of *all fun, no romance,* their new agreement was *take it slow, no rushing things.* An easy yes.

A few months later, she found herself leaving Hadley in charge of the shop more often so she could get away to see Max.

Apparently, this was what taking it slow meant. Even Grams noticed the change.

"Is it just me, or are you coming home more?" she teased, then elbowed Mila in the ribs. "Isn't it about time you opened a shop here?"

Grams had helped her pay her overdue bills, so money was no longer an issue.

That's when she'd decided to open a second shop and leave the Chicago location under Hadley's supervision. Grams was more than thrilled to loan her the money for the second store with the agreement that Mila would move back to Wild Harbor.

Mila didn't even have to think twice.

The winter festival had been such a success for the town that brides were already booking weddings for the following Christmas season. With year-round business, her new store could have an entirely different outcome than her first attempt.

She'd signed the papers to buy the Baker store that day, and her mind whirled with plans for the future.

She turned to admire the storefront again and exhaled deeply, dreaming of the beautiful dresses that would grace the display windows.

"That's not the only surprise today," Max whispered in her ear, causing shivers to erupt down her arms. "Close your eyes."

"Why?" She shut her eyes but was dying to peek at Max's surprise.

"If I told you that, it wouldn't be a surprise. Now turn around slowly and open your eyes."

When she spun around, Max was down on one knee,

holding a velvet jewelry box in his hand.

"Now that you're coming home to Wild Harbor, will you marry me? I want to start a life with you here. There's no one else I'd rather grow old with than you."

Mila covered her mouth with her hands and shook her head in disbelief. "I can't believe you're asking me here. *Now*."

"Are you going to answer me or leave me kneeling in the middle of the sidewalk?" Max teased.

"Yes, yes, of course I will!" She threw her arms around him and nearly toppled him with kisses. He slid the elegant round diamond onto her finger. It shimmered in the light.

"It's beautiful, Max. I can't believe you kept this secret from me."

"My plan to get you back here worked." Max smiled as he wrapped his arms around her and kissed her forehead. "I knew that until you could open a shop here, you wouldn't say yes."

"I *still* would have said yes." Mila would never let her shop get in the way of a future with Max.

"It would have been a more difficult decision. I wanted it to be a no-brainer. A resounding yes. That's why I told you about this building before I asked you to marry me."

"You're a smart man, Max Malone, and you make me exceedingly happy."

"Speaking of weddings, I have a little surprise for you down at the café."

"My favorite caramel latte?"

"Something even better."

Mila took his hand as they strolled down the street. The summer sun warmed her shoulders as she wondered how she'd choose a wedding dress. She'd never asked Cassidy what she'd done with her old dress, and even now, she didn't want to know. The memory of it had burned to ash as soon as she'd handed it to her friend. It had been a strange relief, actually.

When Max opened the door for Mila, she was greeted by a

large crowd shouting, "Surprise!"

Mila stopped, unable to move forward. Max put his arm around her waist and whispered in her ear, "For you, my love."

Joyous faces packed the room. People she had grown up with. Neighbors. Church families. School friends.

"What's going on?" Mila asked incredulously. "How did you all know?"

Diane stepped forward. "Max told us the news ahead of time, and we decided a celebration was in order. The whole town wanted to throw you an engagement party."

"So you planned this for us?" Mila's eyes filled with tears at the news. So many impossible things had happened since she'd arrived home.

This town was now her home again, and Max was going to be her husband. It had all come together in a way she had never expected. A ripple of emotion soared through her, the assurance of knowing this was the path she had waited for all along.

Max wrapped his arms around her and whispered softly in her ear, "Is it everything you ever wanted?"

His touch was like the first sweet sip of a drink she could never grow tired of.

Mila lifted her face to his. "More than you can ever imagine."

Want to experience Alex and Lily's wedding day from Lily's point of view? Download a bonus wedding scene by joining Grace Worthington's newsletter. Get it at graceworthington.com.

Did you love this story? **Leave a review on Amazon!**

Read on for a sneak peek of *The Inn at Wild Harbor.* **Get the book on Amazon.**

THE INN AT WILD HARBOR

SNEAK PEEK OF THE NEXT BOOK IN THE SERIES

Her first rule for a picture-perfect romance: Don't fall for your best friend's brother.

For most of her life, Aspen has hidden her feelings for the striking firefighter who is the older brother of her best friend.

But when she quits her job to pursue photography full-time, she's certain that getting away from her beach town is the answer for moving on with her heart.

It's the perfect plan until her beloved great-aunt dies, leaving Aspen a beautiful inn on the beach. To complicate things, Matt has been living there in return for being the resident security guard and handyman.

Moving in was not part of Aspen's plan, but she's left with no choice. She's broke and needs to sell it.

Despite her best efforts, she can't get away from Matt, but there's no way she'd risk her friendship with him to reveal her true feelings.

It's only when he offers to help her win a photography competition will she consider breaking her first rule of love.

But she's not sure she wants to take a chance with her heart now that her dreams are coming into focus.

Matt has always been tough under pressure. So why did he have a soft spot for Aspen? Despite his attempts to avoid her, their two worlds collide when Aspen inherits the inn.

Now, he's not only living down the hall from her, he's bumping into her at every turn. In the hallway. At breakfast. In the middle of the night. It's enough to make his defenses crumble. But is he brave enough to confess his feelings and compete for her love?

Helping her sell the inn and pursue her dream would be the perfect gift for Aspen.

Except now that he's near her, he doesn't want to let her go.

The Inn at Wild Harbor combines forced proximity, a romance between best friends, and a tough but tender hero to give you a sweet romance story with a happily ever after.

Get The Inn at Wild Harbor on Amazon.

Dear reader,

You are the reason I write. My goal is to help you find a break from real life, to laugh even when life gets heavy, and to remember the joy of falling in love again. I'm grateful that you picked up this book and it's my hope that you loved this story.

To get news about my next book, join my newsletter list at graceworthington.com. I'd love to hear from you!

If you loved *Christmas Wishes in Wild Harbor*, pick up **The Inn at Wild Harbor.**

ACKNOWLEDGMENTS

Many thanks to my husband, who told me I could finish this book before Christmas even when I was convinced I could not. You were right and I was wrong. For once, I'm glad I was. Your encouragement was the push I needed to finish.

I couldn't write books without my dream team. Thanks to my editor, Emily Poole, and my wonderful beta readers, Joy, Heidi, Leigh Ann, Michelle, Thelma, and Denise. Thank you to Judy Zweifel for giving this story a final proofread and Kristen Ingebretson for the fabulous cover design.

To all my readers, thank you.

Love at Wild Harbor

Summer Nights in Wild Harbor

Christmas Wishes in Wild Harbor

The Inn at Wild Harbor

ABOUT THE AUTHOR

Grace Worthington writes Christian fiction and clean contemporary romance novels because she loves giving readers a happily ever after with heart. She has a degree in English and resides with her husband and two children in Indiana.

Did you know there is a bonus wedding epilogue of Lily and Alex's wedding from the bride's point of view? Don't miss the free epilogue.

Sign up for it at graceworthington.com and get notified of sales on Grace's books and other great deals.